Violet's Bumpy Ride

Violet's Bumpy Ride

BOOK SIX

of the
*A Life of Faith:
Violet Travilla*
Series

Based on the characters by
Martha Finley

MCP
Mission City Press

Franklin, Tennessee

Book Six of the *A Life of Faith: Violet Travilla* Series

Violet's Bumpy Ride
Copyright © 2005, Mission City Press, Inc. All Rights Reserved.

Published by Mission City Press, Inc.

This book is based on the *Elsie Dinsmore* series written by Martha Finley and first published in 1868 by Dodd, Mead & Company.

Cover & Interior Design: Richmond & Williams
Cover Photography: Michelle Grisco Photography
Typesetting: BookSetters

Unless otherwise indicated, all Scripture references are from the Holy Bible, New International Version (NIV). Copyright © 1973, 1978, 1984 by International Bible Society. Used by permission of Zondervan Publishing House, Grand Rapids, MI. All rights reserved.

Violet Travilla and *A Life of Faith* are trademarks of Mission City Press, Inc.

For more information, write to Mission City Press at 202 Second Avenue South, Franklin, Tennessee 37064, or visit our Web Site at:

www.alifeoffaith.com

Library of Congress Catalog Card Number: 2005924780
Finley, Martha
     Violet's Bumpy Ride
     Book Six of the *A Life of Faith: Violet Travilla* Series
     ISBN: 1-928749-22-4

Printed in the United States of America
1 2 3 4 5 6 7 8 — 10 09 08 07 06 05

—FOREWORD—

*L*ife is certainly full for Violet Travilla! Her inner city mission has survived the vicious schemes of those who wanted to destroy it. The good people of Wildwood have put aside their suspicions and welcomed Samaritan House into their community. Already, the mission is adding new services, and Vi and her friends have plans for more changes to improve life in their poor community. Big changes also lie ahead for Vi herself, but unknown to her, a problem is brewing that could dash her hopes for happiness.

Violet's Bumpy Ride is the sixth volume in the *A Life of Faith: Violet Travilla* series, based on characters created by Martha Finley in the second half of the nineteenth century. Miss Finley wrote for the young people of her own time, yet her message of faith in the Lord's saving grace as the precious cornerstone of every life remains as powerful today as ever.

∾ THE VICTORIAN PANTRY ∾

Cooks in Violet's time were key participants in a revolution. This Victorian kitchen revolution resulted from the Industrial Revolution, which made it possible to mass produce food products and dramatically change home cooking with the invention of new "labor-saving" devices.

At first glance, the kitchen in a middleclass city home in the late 1800s and early 1900s would seem plain and bare to a visitor from our century. No microwave, no dishwasher, no

electric gadgets, and no refrigerator or freezer! But a closer look would reveal all the basic tools that cooks today rely on. Biscuits or a beef roast might be baking in the oven. A pot of soup might be bubbling on the wood-burning or gas range. (Electric stoves, introduced in the 1880s, were still too unreliable for most cooks.) The middle class cook's array of utensils might include new, lighter-weight aluminum pots and pans. She would wash up in a porcelain or metal sink supplied with water from a faucet or tap (replacing hand-operated water pumps). At the end of the day, she'd mop her colorful linoleum kitchen floor—a new invention that was easier to clean than wood planking or stone.

Milk, butter, and meats would be kept in the icebox—a large wooden box, lined inside with sheet metal and chilled by a solid block of ice purchased from a commercial ice house. On a summer afternoon, the modern-day visitor might notice someone cranking the handle of a deep wooden tub packed with chunks of ice—the making of ice cream. The visitor might also see a large barrel-shaped tub on legs—the washing machine in which linens and clothing were churned in soapy water. The machine was filled with hand-drawn buckets of water and cranked by hand, a task that required strong arms and backs.

The shelves of the kitchen pantry might be stocked with products familiar to cooks of today: cans of Campbell's condensed tomato soup, Log Cabin syrup, Wesson oil, and Borden's condensed milk; tin boxes of Premium soda crackers and Triscuits; bags of Pillsbury flour, Quaker oats, Aunt Jemima pancake mix, Post and Kellogg's cereals; and canned goods with brand names like Del Monte, Libby, and Armours. The pantry might include McCormick spices, Lipton tea, Calumet baking powder, Knox gelatin, and Nabisco graham crackers.

By the last quarter of the nineteenth century, manufactured food products were enabling American cooks to serve more varied menus. Cooks were no longer limited to the fruits and vegetables in season in their locale. With industrial canning and bottling, even exotic foods, like pineapple, became affordable for the middle class and could be served year-round.

Food safety was a serious concern, and some of the early, experimental methods for sterilizing, preserving, and canning foods were downright deadly. But it was an age of invention and scientific discovery, and improvements in food processing and packaging came rapidly. The first canned foods were sealed in large, tin-plated iron drums, which had to be opened with a hammer and chisel! A Connecticut inventor patented a clumsy can opener in 1858, but the forerunner of modern can openers came in 1870. William Lyman's innovation—a wheeled blade that cut around the edge of the tin can—made it possible for ordinary cooks to easily use canned foods.

Heavy advertising sold Americans on the convenience of processed foods. Food ads commonly featured happy housewives and children and sold the health benefits (often exaggerated), speed of preparation, and low costs of processed food products.

Some of the foods, brand names, and food trends that come to us from the late 1800s and early 1900s include:

Potato chips—George Crum, a Native American, "invented" potato chips in 1853. As a chef in Saratoga Springs, New York, he served wafer-thin, fried potato

slices to a diner who complained that his French fries were too thick. Hand-sliced "Saratoga chips" were sold mostly in New England, until mechanical peeling and slicing machines made it possible to produce chips for mass consumption.

Popping corn — The Indians of the Americas perfected the art of popping corn kernels thousands of years ago. But it wasn't easy to pop corn until the development of popping machines in the 1880s.

F. W. Rueckheim and his brother, both German immigrants, combined popcorn and peanuts, coated in molasses, and introduced what would later be named Cracker Jacks at the 1893 World's Fair.

Peanut butter — A spread made from peanuts was developed in the 1890s, when a St. Louis doctor asked a local food maker to process peanut paste as a source of protein for people with chewing difficulties. In 1895, Dr. John Harvey Kellogg of Michigan patented a "Process of Preparing Nut Meal." Peanut butter was first sold at the 1904 St. Louis World's Fair, but the first manufacturer was the Krema company of Ohio.

Hot dogs — In 1852, butchers in Frankfurt, Germany created a spicy, curved frankfurter sausage, which was introduced to America by German immigrants in the 1880s. Served on a roll, the frankfurter, which the Germans nicknamed the "dashshund sausage," soon became the all-American hot dog. R. T. French, a manufacturer of spices, introduced a creamy, yellow mustard at the 1904 St. Louis World's Fair, and it became a favorite dressing for hot dogs.

Foreword

Hamburger—Ground or chopped meat was eaten at least as early as the Middle Ages. In Germany, poor people added spices to shredded beef and served it cooked or raw. Known as "Hamburg steak" for the city of Hamburg, this popular meat dish was brought to America by German immigrants in the 1880s. No one knows when hamburgers were first put on buns, but that's how they were sold at the 1904 St. Louis World's Fair.

Tomato ketchup—The word comes from Malaysia, where a sauce based on a seventeenth century Chinese recipe was called kechap. Tomatoes were added to the recipe in America near the end of the 1700s. Cooks made their own ketchup, but it was an arduous task. So when Henry Heinz began selling bottled ketchup in 1876, it was an immediate success. Heinz added pickles and other spicy sauces to his product line and coined the slogan "57 Varieties."

Other still-popular condiments include A.1. Steak Sauce, created by the chef to King George IV of England; Worcestershire Sauce, a recipe from India, first bottled in England by chemists John Lea and William Perrins in the mid-1880s; and Tabasco Sauce, a hot pepper sauce invented by New Orleans banker Edmund McIlhenny and first sold in the U.S. in 1868.

Pancake mix—In early Christian tradition, pancakes were eaten on Shrove Tuesday, the day before the start of the Lenten season. The ingredients were symbolic: flour represented the staff of life, eggs symbolized rebirth, and milk stood for innocence. The Pilgrims called pancakes "no cake"—the source of the term "hoe cake." In 1889, St.

Violet's Bumpy Ride

Joseph newspaper reporter Chris L. Rutt packed flour, soda, lime phosphate, and salt in paper bags. His pancake mix didn't sell well until Rutt named it "Aunt Jemima" after a vaudeville song and used the image of an African-American woman on the packages.

Soft drinks – People have made herb-based drinks for centuries, but pharmacist Charles Hires turned root beer into a commercial success by improving the taste. Hires's root beer was first sold at the 1876 Philadelphia Centennial Exposition. Dr. Pepper, invented by pharmacist Charles Alderton in 1885, holds the title of oldest major manufacturer of soft drinks in the U.S. A year later, another pharmacist, John Stith Pemberton of Atlanta, concocted his recipe for Coca-Cola. Soft drinks, or soda pop, were sold at soda fountains (many located in drugstores) where the drink syrup could be mixed with carbonated water. With the development of mechanical bottle-capping in the early 1890s, the fizzy drinks could be bottled. Brands like Canada Dry, Pepsi, and Royal Crown arrived in the early 1900s.

Animal crackers – Animal-shaped cookies, first sold in England in the 1890s, were introduced to American children in 1902 by the National Biscuit Company (a cooperative of bakeries that became Nabisco). The cookies were named "Barnum's Cookies" for P.T Barnum, a famous showman, and sold in colorful circus-themed cardboard boxes.

Jello—In 1897, Pearl B. Wait, a cough syrup maker from LeRoy, New York, developed a flavored, powdered gelatin, and his wife, Mary, came up with the catchy name "Jell-O." The product had a slow start, but by 1906, Americans were buying $1 million worth of Jell-O each year. The original flavors were strawberry, lemon, orange, and raspberry.

Not everybody could afford these new convenience foods, and the meals of the poor and working classes were very limited in content and quantity. Efforts to assist the poor around the turn of the century began to include education in the preparation of low-cost, healthy meals. Scientific research in human nutrition led to the emergence of "home economics" as a legitimate profession.

Kitchen pantries in rural America might include a few packaged foods, but farm cooks depended on the foods they grew and preserved themselves. People in the South and Southwest probably ate more fresh foods, because their climate allowed longer growing seasons. It wasn't until the full-scale extension of electric power into rural areas, beginning in 1935, that country dwellers could easily enjoy the convenience of processed foods and modern appliances—a kitchen revolution begun in America's cities more than fifty years earlier.

Travilla/Dinsmore Family Tree

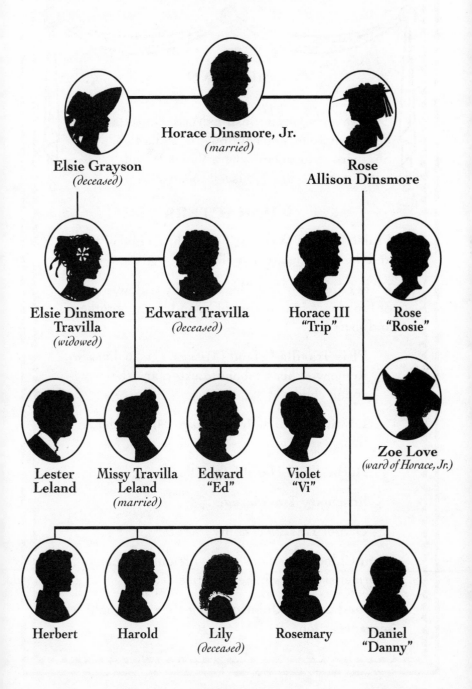

SETTING

*T*he story begins in Boston, Massachusetts, in February, 1884, and continues to India Bay, the Southern seaport city where Violet Travilla's mission, Samaritan House, is located.

CHARACTERS

Violet Travilla (Vi), age 20, the third child of Elsie and the late Edward Travilla.

Elsie Dinsmore Travilla, a wealthy widow, owner of Ion plantation; mother of Vi and her six brothers and sisters:

> **Elsie Travilla Leland (Missy)**, age 26; lives in Rome with her husband, **Lester**, and their young child.

> **Edward Travilla, Jr. (Ed)**, age 24; manager of Ion.

> **Herbert and Harold Travilla**, twins, age 18

> **Rosemary Travilla**, age 13

> **Daniel Travilla (Danny)**, age 9

Aunt Chloe, Elsie Dinsmore's lifelong companion; a former slave now in her eighties.

Ben and Crystal Johnson, long-time household servants at Ion.

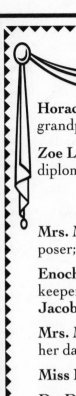

Horace Dinsmore, Jr. and his wife, **Rose**, Vi's grandparents and owners of The Oaks plantation.

Zoe Love, age 19, daughter of a deceased American diplomat and ward of Horace Dinsmore, Jr.

∽ Samaritan House ∽

Mrs. Maurene O'Flaherty, widow of a famous composer; Vi's companion and friend.

Enoch and Christine Reeve, caretaker and housekeeper at Samaritan House, and their young son, **Jacob**.

Mrs. Mary Appleton, Samaritan House's cook, and her daughter, **Polly**, age 6.

Miss Emily Clayton, a nurse.

Dr. David Bowman, a physician.

Tansy Evans, age 11, and **Marigold**, age 6, orphaned sisters who live at Samaritan House.

Miss Alma Hansen, a young seamstress.

∽ Others ∽

Mark Raymond, a college professor and archaeologist; widowed father of three children:

    Max, age 11

    Lucilla (Lulu), almost age 10

    Grace (Gracie), almost age 6

Miss Gertrude Marsh (Aunt Gert), the Raymond children's great-aunt and caretaker.

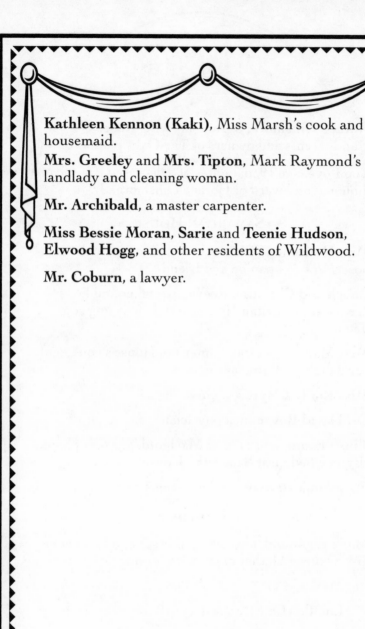

Kathleen Kennon (Kaki), Miss Marsh's cook and housemaid.

Mrs. Greeley and **Mrs. Tipton**, Mark Raymond's landlady and cleaning woman.

Mr. Archibald, a master carpenter.

Miss Bessie Moran, **Sarie** and **Teenie Hudson**, **Elwood Hogg**, and other residents of Wildwood.

Mr. Coburn, a lawyer.

CHAPTER

1

Three Children

*Men do not despise a thief
if he steals to satisfy his
hunger when he is
starving.*

PROVERBS 6:30

Three Children

hat's that in your hand?" Max Raymond demanded of Lulu.

He had come across his sister as he rounded the corner of the woodshed behind the gloomy Boston townhouse where they lived. It was a cold February day, and Max was surprised to find his sister outside. She jumped when he spoke to her, and Max saw that she was even more surprised than he.

"Keep your voice down," Lulu whispered fiercely. Then her mouth widened into a bright and slightly crooked smile, and she extended her hand to show her brother what it held. "It's the pantry key. I'm going to get us some food."

"You stole that from Aunt Gert?" he asked incredulously.

"I did not!" his younger sister replied emphatically. "I found it. It's Auntie's extra key. It was just lying on the kitchen table for anyone to use. So I'm going to use it."

Max looked unconvinced.

"You know Aunt Gert didn't leave that key for you, Lulu," he said. "She doesn't allow us in the food pantry."

Lulu Raymond scrunched her eyebrows into an angry V and narrowed her eyes to slits. She drew in a breath, puffed her cheeks so that her freckles seemed to stand out, and puckered her lips into a tight knot. Max knew that look well: it was Lulu's "mad face," and he always thought it funny, though he never dared say so to his sister.

Instead he said, "Don't get in a temper, Lulu. I know you wouldn't steal the key."

Lulu expelled the air in her cheeks and said, "I *borrowed* the key. It's just the spare key that's usually on the hook. As

soon as Aunt Gert goes out today, I'll use it to get some real food for you and Gracie and me. Then I'll put the key back. That's not stealing. The food belongs to us 'cause Papa has paid for it. He wants us to have good food—not Aunt Gert's disgusting corn mush and cabbage and bitter tea."

"I know," Max conceded with a sigh. "But Aunt Gert thinks it's good for us. She read about it in one of those magazines of hers. She says meat and milk and eggs are bad for children, that they'll make us sluggish and dull our brains."

"Well, she's wrong," Lulu said with another frown. "Mush and tea are no better for us than the other stupid things she's made us eat since we came here. Remember the time we got only chicken wings and fish? She didn't care if we ate meat then. Besides, nothing but mush and tea is making Gracie sick. I'm going to get her some real food, and that's that!"

Max had to agree. He was an honorable boy, and he didn't like the idea of "borrowing" the key. But he was as worried as Lulu about their little sister. Gracie had always been somewhat frail and was smaller than most girls her age, which was nearly six. Recently she'd become weaker—sometimes so weak that she could barely stand. The children's aunt, Miss Gertrude Marsh (great-aunt really, for the lady was in actuality the aunt of their late mother) didn't seem especially concerned about Gracie's condition. In fact, Miss Marsh had said that Gracie's thin frame and sallow complexion were attractive in a girl. That was just one of Miss Marsh's many strange ideas.

"I know," Max said. "But aren't you afraid you'll get caught? Kaki is sure to see that the food is gone," he cautioned, referring to the young servant who lived in the house and cooked and cleaned for Miss Marsh.

"Oh, pooh," Lulu declared. "Kaki won't tell. She's worried about Gracie, too."

"I wish Papa were here," Max said. "He'd see what's happening and fix everything."

"But he wouldn't see," Lulu said in a sorrowful tone. "Whenever he visits, Aunt Gert treats us just like other children. We have good food, and you don't have to do all those awful chores. She's even nice to me when Papa's around. I wanted to tell him the truth when he came for Christmas. But he had such a lot on his mind. Now we won't see him again till summer, and—and—and Gracie could be dead by then!"

"Don't say that!" Max returned with uncharacteristic hardness. "Don't ever say that. Gracie would be as strong as you and me if she had some healthy food."

In a softer tone, he went on, "Okay, you *borrowed* the spare key. And Papa has always told us to take care of Gracie. It's not exactly right to take food, but it would be wrong to let Gracie starve. I'll help you."

Lulu's eyes opened wide, and she exclaimed, "No, you can't! If Auntie catches you, she'll put you in the attic again. And you'll get the pea-monia or something else terrible!"

"She'll do the same to you," Max laughed.

"No, she won't," Lulu replied. "She'll get all whiny and tell me I'm hopeless like she always does. She'll send me to bed without supper. But I'm a girl, so she won't make me sleep in that freezing attic."

That was true. Miss Marsh had never taken care of children until the three young Raymonds came to live with her when she was well into her middle age. She'd been prejudiced against Max from the start. The children had finally realized that their great-aunt just didn't like any boys very much. She often quoted the rhyme that boys were "snakes and snails and puppy dog tails" but girls were "sugar and spice and everything nice."

Though just seven years old when he went to live in his aunt's house, Max had immediately been assigned chores fit for grown boys and men, and he was given harsh punishments whenever he offended his aunt. Gracie was her favorite, largely because the youngest Raymond was by nature a compliant and agreeable child. Max, now eleven, was much like Gracie in his general character, for he rarely became angry and tried his best to comply with his aunt's strange rules. The trouble was that Miss Marsh was so unpredictable that the rules were constantly changing.

Only Lulu, who was nearly ten, rebelled against their aunt's authority, and she did so with regularity. A keen and sensitive observer of the scene would have seen that Lulu's rebellious words and deeds were almost always in defense of her brother or her sister. Sometimes, when Max was about to be punished unfairly for some minor thing—like having dirty fingernails at the breakfast table because Miss Marsh had made him shovel coal—Lulu would suddenly and rudely sass her aunt about a wholly different matter. Or she might cause some commotion by spilling or even breaking something and then arguing loudly with her aunt about whether it was done by accident or with deliberation. In the end, Lulu would admit her guilt and accept punishment for such naughty deeds without too much grumbling. But her outbursts often distracted Miss Marsh's attention and saved Max from anything worse than a hasty reprimand.

Lulu herself did not consciously connect her behavior with her instinct to protect her siblings, for she really believed that she was, as her aunt told her nearly every day, a naughty, willful, and evil-tempered child.

"At least I can be your lookout," Max was saying. "You can get the food while Aunt Gert is out and Kaki is cleaning upstairs. I'll warn you if either of them is coming."

"That's alright, I guess," Lulu said thoughtfully.

"Go back to the house before Aunt Gert knows you're out here," Max said. "I have to cut kindling, and Auntie will be mad if she thinks I'm talking instead of working."

Slipping the pantry key into her coat pocket, Lulu poked her brother playfully on his arm and then trudged back to the house.

Gertrude Marsh did not think it cruel to deprive her nieces and nephew of hearty foods. She genuinely believed that she was doing her best. She was the kind of person who liked to talk about "scientific theories" and "modern methods." She read cheap magazines and advertising pamphlets and went to lectures and meetings on all sorts of bizarre topics.

What Miss Marsh lacked was a mind of her own. She was susceptible to any new idea—the latest inventions, the newest patent cure-all medicines, the most outrageous "health" fads including the diets to which she subjected the Raymond children. Her addiction to "new ideas" was the chief reason why her rules for the children were so capricious, changing without rhyme or reason from week to week and sometimes day to day and leaving Lulu and Max in a constant state of befuddlement.

Their aunt was not an unkind woman—even Lulu had to admit that. Miss Marsh doted on Gracie and provided her with the finest clothing and nicest toys. She fretted endlessly about Gracie's "delicacy," keeping the child mostly indoors and denying her the fresh air and physical activity that might have strengthened a weak constitution. She undertook Gracie's intellectual and moral education herself, though Max and Lulu were enrolled in the local primary school and Sunday school. It never occurred to Miss Marsh that Gracie might get stronger with a healthy diet, exercise, and the opportunity to play as other children did.

Miss Marsh's negative attitude toward Max resulted from the fact that she had hardly ever been around boys in her life. Her father had been a cold and distant man with little apparent interest in his two children, both daughters, except to keep them away from the influence of other children. Miss Marsh, who never married, had not even been allowed a social life in her girlhood and no suitors when she was a young woman.

When her parents died, Miss Marsh inherited the family house. Though she'd added modern conveniences over the years, she kept the house looking almost exactly as it did in her parents' time, which accounted for its dark, heavy furnishings; shuttered and draped windows; and altogether dismal aspect. Until the arrival of Max, Lulu, and Gracie, she'd been content to keep the large townhouse in its shrine-like condition and indulge the whimsical side of her personality in the pursuit of "new ideas."

The children knew very little of their aunt's history. Max, who had clear memories of his loving and clever mother, wondered why his great-aunt was so strange and flighty but did everything he could to please her. Gracie, who was only two when her mother died and too young to remember anything, accepted her aunt's odd ways without question. Lulu remembered their mother, though not with Max's clarity. So in her mind, Lulu created an idealized picture of her mother, and she resented her great-aunt all the more because the woman could not live up to the perfection of this ideal.

The children all adored their Papa and treasured his every visit with them. But they really didn't know him very well, and when they were with him, they all pretended to be completely happy. Yet in their hearts, all three children longed for the day when he would rescue them from the dark house near Beacon Hill and reunite their little family.

Lulu was on her best behavior around her aunt all that morning, and she ate her meager, tasteless lunch without complaint, even though her aunt was enjoying a nice piece of steak for her own meal.

Soon after lunch, Miss Marsh left to attend a lecture that would keep her away from the house all the afternoon. Before departing, she assigned Max a series of tasks that would occupy him until her return and told Lulu and Gracie to work at their sewing until time for Gracie's nap.

When their aunt had gone, Max went outside to his work, and Lulu and Gracie climbed the house's dreary front staircase to Gracie's little bedroom, which connected to their aunt's room. Lulu immediately yanked open the dark curtains and threw back the shutters that covered the windows.

"I bet bears' caves are brighter than this old house!" she declared in disgust. "The whole time we've lived here, nobody's ever opened a window to let in the breezes."

Gracie, who had settled into a little rocking chair by the fireplace, said softly, "Aunt Gert says there are things in the outside air that will make us sick. She says the air in the city is bad for children."

Lulu pouted and said, "If that's true, then Max ought to be very sick. Aunt Gert sends him outside all the time. He has to chop wood and sweep the paths and cut the hedges, and he's healthy."

"But Aunt Gert says he's strong because he's a boy," Gracie stated.

"I know what Aunt Gert says," Lulu replied with a disheartened sigh. "She told us to sew, but I have another idea. You sew, and I'll read us that new storybook you have."

"I'd like that," Gracie said, a smile enlivening her pale face. "But Auntie will be mad if you don't do your sewing. She said for you to mend the hem on that pillowcase." Gracie pointed to a white item that lay on her bed.

"I'll get it done," Lulu replied. "But let me read first. I can do that hem while you have your nap."

Gracie had taken up a small hoop from the table beside her chair. She began making careful stitches on the cloth stretched across the hoop. For one so young, she was very good at her needlework, and her great-aunt was currently teaching her simple embroidery.

"I guess that's alright," Gracie agreed. "But you gotta do your work. I don't want you in trouble again."

"I promise I will," Lulu said with a laugh. "Now, where's that book?"

The two sisters passed their time together in the most pleasant companionship. Gracie loved it when Lulu read aloud, for Lulu didn't just say the words, as Aunt Gert did. Lulu *acted* the stories with flair, using different voices for the characters and reading with such drama that the action seemed real.

Lulu had just finished the third story in the book when there was a knock at the door and Kaki came in.

"Time for you to sleep now, Miss Gracie," the young woman said in her thick Irish accent. "Miss Marsh'll have me head if I let you miss your nap."

Gracie never disobeyed her aunt's instructions, so she put her embroidery aside and went to her narrow bed, snuggling down on her pillow while Kaki gently tucked a warm quilt around her.

"Sleep now, little one," Kaki said in a soft tone as she ran her hand gently over Gracie's forehead. "Sleep well."

Gracie, who tired so easily, closed her eyes and almost instantly drifted off.

Lulu and Kaki slipped quietly from the room. In the hall, Lulu spoke to the maid in a whisper, saying, "You are really good to Gracie."

"That's not hard," Kaki said kindly. "I wish I could do more for her, but —"

She stopped herself suddenly and became very businesslike in manner. "But I've got me work to do," she resumed briskly. "Miss Marsh wants the spare room cleaned out. She'll have me head if it ain't done when she gets back. You best do that sewing of yours, or Miss Marsh'll have your head too."

With this warning, Kaki walked off to collect the broom and dusters she'd left beside the staircase. Gathering her skirts, she climbed the stairs to the third floor.

Lulu listened until she no longer heard Kaki's footsteps. The girl wondered what Kaki had been about to say, but she didn't give it much thought. She was glad the maid

hadn't asked what she planned to do, for Lulu would not have been untruthful. She was sure that Kaki would have agreed to her plan to get food for Gracie, but Lulu had no desire to involve anyone in her actions: if someone got in trouble, it would be she alone.

Lulu hurried downstairs, making as little noise as possible, and went to the kitchen. Her winter coat was hanging on a peg near the rear door, and she took the "borrowed" key from its pocket. Her hands were shaking as she opened the pantry door.

The pantry was a narrow room, like a closet but deeper. Shelves ran down one side of the room. There were hooks on the other side, where Kaki hung her coat and clean aprons. Mops and buckets, another broom, a carpet sweeper, and a stepladder stood against the back wall.

There was no light in the pantry, so Lulu left the door open. She scanned the shelves, quickly deciding what she could take without arousing her aunt's suspicion. She grabbed two cans of peaches and a small pot of jam. She took three fat pickles from a jar and wrapped them in a bit of brown paper from the stack of old papers that her Aunt Gert saved. Then she looked in the breadbox and found a whole loaf of fresh bread. But she ignored the bread, taking instead a tin of crackers, which was half full.

She saw a plate covered with a towel, and under the towel was a large piece of cooked steak from which her aunt's luncheon had been cut. The aroma of the meat was incredibly delicious for a young girl who had eaten only mush and boiled cabbage for the last month or so. She would gladly have endured any punishment just for a taste.

She took the plate into the kitchen, and finding a clean knife, she sliced two pieces off the steak. She cut the smaller piece into little bites for Gracie, leaving the larger piece whole since it was intended for Max. Then she studied the steak for several moments. No, she decided, she wouldn't cut any for herself; if she took too much, her aunt would know. Instead, she wrapped the meat in a napkin, took the plate back to the pantry shelf, and carefully replaced the towel. *Maybe Aunt Gert won't notice what's missing*, Lulu told herself hopefully, as she washed the knife and put it back in its place.

She scrounged in a drawer for an old can opener and a couple of spoons; then she tumbled all the items she'd gathered into a little basket with a broken handle. She was anxious to leave the kitchen but remembered to lock the pantry and hang the key on the hook where it usually rested when her aunt or Kaki wasn't around.

Running up the stairs to her own bedroom, Lulu shoved the basket of food under her bed and hurried to Gracie's room. She entered on tiptoe, found the pillowcase that she was supposed to hem, and sat down on the rug beside the fireplace. A needle and thread were stuck in the fabric, and Lulu set to work. Her hands were still shaking. Her stitches were too long, and she didn't bother to keep the thread untwisted. But she was determined to finish the work and keep her promise to Gracie.

The little girl was still sleeping peacefully, her thumb in her mouth. Gracie's soft breathing was the only sound in the room, and it calmed Lulu's pounding heart and trembling hands. Though she didn't notice, her stitches became smoother and more even as she progressed. Her mind, however, was racing. She was sure that, sooner or later, her

aunt would find out what she'd done, and she was prepared to take full blame and accept whatever punishment came along. She just wanted to get the food to Gracie and Max before the inevitable discovery of her actions.

Lulu finished the hemming and was tying a knot in the thread when Max opened the door.

"No sign of Auntie," he whispered. "Did you do it?"

"Yes," Lulu replied, scrambling up and dropping the pillowcase on the floor.

Pointing to their sleeping sister, Lulu went to the door and motioned for Max to go with her to her room. Once inside, she retrieved the basket and set it on her bedside table. As she displayed each item for Max, his mouth began to water. He had become so used to being hungry that he'd almost forgotten how real food might taste.

He took a pickle and bit into it greedily. The juice ran down his chin.

"Don't eat too fast," Lulu warned, "or you'll get sick."

"I won't," Max mumbled as he chewed.

Lulu opened a napkin and held out the steak. At the sight, Max's eyes sparkled with pleasure.

Lulu said, "The big piece is for you. Gracie and I'll share the rest."

Ten minutes later, Max was licking the last of the pickle juice from his fingers and looking satisfied. Steak and pickle, with crackers and jam for dessert—it was more of a meal than he had had for a very long time.

"Take a can of peaches for later," Lulu told him. "You could hide it in the shed."

"And open it with my axe," he laughed as he shoved the can and one of the spoons into his jacket pocket. "That'll be a lot more fun than chopping firewood."

Three Children

"Peaches will taste better'n Aunt Gert's fish oil," Lulu said, shivering at the thought of the nightly doses of cod-liver oil that her aunt administered without fail.

Lulu left her room for a few moments, returning to report that Gracie was waking.

"Kaki's still upstairs. You gotta go down and watch out for Auntie," Lulu said. "I'll get Gracie to eat."

Encouraging Gracie to share the food was more difficult than Lulu expected. Gracie knew that Aunt Gert allowed no eating between meals, and she couldn't understand why Lulu was offering her something that was forbidden.

"Is Papa coming?" Gracie asked, remembering that meat and fruit were only served when their father was visiting.

"No, but he'd want you to have this," Lulu replied. "He gives Aunt Gert lots of money for us, and he'd be mad if he knew how she feeds us mush and cabbage."

"But Aunt Gert says it's good for us," Gracie protested. "She wants us to be healthy."

Lulu almost responded with angry words against their aunt, but she restrained her impulse. "Aunt Gert doesn't understand children," she said. "Children need good food to grow strong. Won't you try a bite of steak?"

Reluctantly, Gracie did take a small piece of steak. "It's good," she said.

She ate another piece and then a cracker spread with jam. Lulu was about to open the can of peaches, when she saw an odd look on her sister's face.

"I can't eat more," Gracie said plaintively. "It feels funny in my stomach."

"That's 'cause you're not used to it," Lulu said. "You can have more later. I'll keep the basket in my room."

"Aunt Gert'll be mad," Gracie said.

"Don't worry about Aunt Gert," Lulu responded, forcing herself to laugh.

"I'm scared for you," Gracie said, tears welling in her large blue eyes.

"I haven't done anything wrong," Lulu said. "Remember that Papa paid for this food. He wants us to have it."

"Will you tell him?" Gracie asked.

"Of course I will," Lulu said firmly. "I'll tell him the next time he comes. I'll tell him everything, and maybe he'll take us away to live with him, and we'll be a real family."

This brought a bright smile to Gracie's face. "I'd like that," she said. "Auntie is nice, but I'd like to be with our Papa all the time."

"Me too," Lulu said softly, as she put the remaining food back in the basket. "Let me take this to my room. Then we'll go find Max. Maybe he'll play the piano for us before Auntie comes back."

"That would be nice," Gracie said, her thoughts shifting to the prospect of being with her brother and sister. She always enjoyed the lively music that Max played when their great-aunt wasn't around.

Lulu's thoughts were going in a different direction. Would she really tell her Papa what she'd done that day (and hoped to do again)? She decided that she would, even if he was terribly mad at her—even if knowing that she'd taken food against her aunt's wishes made him not love her. That was Lulu's greatest fear. It was the reason she'd never before complained to him about their Aunt Gert. If her father really knew what a rebellious and bad-tempered child she was, how could he love her?

Three Children

Lulu wished that she could be like Gracie, who was so sweet and never caused trouble for anyone. Or like Max, who seemed able to accept things that infuriated Lulu and who tried to find the good in every situation. But Lulu was Lulu—with an overwhelming sense of fairness, intense loyalty to her siblings, and a volatile temper that often goaded her to act against her own best interests.

Could she live without her father's love? She told herself that she could, if that was the price of getting Max and Gracie away from Aunt Gert and her gloomy house and of saving Gracie from starvation.

So Lulu decided to speak up when her father came again in June. It was such a long time to wait, more than three months. But until he returned, she'd steal food (yes, she admitted to herself, that was what she'd done, even if the food was rightfully theirs) and do whatever else she must to protect her brother and sister. Then she'd tell her father the truth. And if he hated her, she'd go far, far away. The idea of being alone terrified her. But maybe her father would understand. Maybe when he knew the truth, he would see what she saw every time she looked into Gracie's pale, thin face. And maybe, just maybe, he would forgive his sinful elder daughter.

CHAPTER

2

In the Nick of Time

For he has rescued us from the dominion of darkness and brought us into the kingdom of the Son he loves. . . .

COLOSSIANS 1:13

rofessor Mark Raymond was star-
ing out the window of the speeding train
and smiling to himself. His eyes seemed
riveted on the snow-covered landscape
passing by, but in fact, another vision
filled his imagination.

He saw a small office in an old house.
An open rolltop desk was cluttered with papers. A window
curtained in white lace looked out on a side garden where
bare maple trees would soon begin to bud. An orange cat
stretched out on the windowsill and lazily lapped at her
paw. At the desk sat the true object of his daydream—a
lean and lovely young woman whose dark hair gleamed in
the winter sunlight. A few strands had come loose from
their pins and dangled against her willowy neck. She was
concentrating on something and twisting a pair of eyeglasses in her long, elegant fingers. At any moment, Mark
thought, she'll look up, and her dimpled smile will fill the
room with brightness.

The professor laughed at his imaginings and turned his
head away from the window. How dramatically his plans had
changed since he last laid eyes on Vi just four days earlier.
Departing from India Bay on the previous Friday, he'd
arrived in his Eastern university town of Kingstown the next
night and gone directly to his living quarters. But he'd stayed
in his apartment only long enough to write a note to his
cleaning lady and repack his traveling bag. Returning to the
depot, he'd purchased a ticket for the next train to Boston,
which left at dawn on Sunday morning. He'd spent the night
on a bench in the depot's waiting area, napping occasionally
but mostly contemplating what lay ahead of him.

Violet's Bumpy Ride

He had sent two telegrams, copies of which he now held in his hand. One was to Miss Gertrude Marsh in Boston — a brief message telling her of his imminent arrival and asking her to inform his children.

The second telegram was addressed to Miss Violet Travilla, Samaritan House, Wildwood Street, India Bay. It read:

> *Going to Boston today. Keep the children and me in your prayers.*
> *Courtship is the right word. Do you agree?*
> *Mark*

The message seemed so terse, but he knew that Vi would understand his meaning. When he'd seen Vi on the day before leaving India Bay, he had only asked permission to call on her when he returned to the Southern city where he hoped to make his new home. "Courtship," he'd told her, was something for future consideration, when they both knew their feelings better. Yet within an hour of saying good-bye to Vi, he knew that he would court her, and if she returned his affection, he would marry her and love her till the last moment of his life.

There would be difficulties. He'd gone over the problems again and again. First and foremost — his three children. In his grief over the death of his wife, he had all but abandoned them. He'd told himself that it was for their good, but now he understood that he had acted from selfishness. Without even being aware of her influence on him, Vi had opened his eyes as well as his heart again, and he was determined to make amends to his beloved Max and

22

Lulu and Gracie. But he could not be sure if they would want him in their lives as more than an infrequent visitor or how they would react to the idea of a new mamma. He loved Vi, but would they?

There was also his career. He had been offered a position as the head of the classical languages department at India Bay University, and he hoped to move his children to the South, where they could live together at last. He could be with his family, teaching his university classes and coming home to his wife (he prayed this would be so) and children just as other husbands and fathers did every day. But the professor was also an archaeologist, and his work would often take him away from his family. He could be absent for months, exploring in remote locations and entirely beyond contact with his loved ones. If Vi agreed to marry him, would she be prepared to be sole parent to his three youngsters during these periods?

And how would Vi's family take his courtship? Mark was a friend of the Travillas and always welcome in their home. But as a son-in-law and brother-in-law? That was an entirely different matter. He was twelve years older than Vi, a widower with three children. He could certainly support his family, but he could offer Vi none of the wealth she had grown up in. That, he knew, was of little matter to her; she was perhaps the least materialistic and most generous woman he'd ever met. She would, however, inherit a great fortune, and Mark worried about how it might complicate their lives.

He'd been thinking and praying over all these things and more for weeks, and at times he had despaired. Now, after his last meeting with Vi, it seemed that together, they could find solutions to every problem. All except Mark's

relationship with his children. Vi's words had given him strength and courage, but only he could repair the damage he'd caused by his callous behavior.

He looked again at the messages in his hand; then he placed the sheets in his travel case and leaned back against the seat with a sigh. How would Max, Lulu, and Gracie receive him? How would they feel about the possibility of moving to India Bay and making their home with him there? They'd always seemed so happy to be in Boston with their Aunt Gert. Did he have the right to ask them to make a break with the only home they'd known for the last four years? They would need time to consider, and he must be patient. If they decided not to make the change he proposed, he had to be understanding.

Mark knew himself well enough to realize that patience and understanding were not his strongest characteristics. He closed his eyes and offered up a prayer, seeking the Lord's guidance and asking for His help. Then, as the railway car rocked and rattled its way to Boston, he fell into a restless sleep, and his dreams were filled with the faces of his three children.

It was rather late in the evening when Mark Raymond reached his destination. He considered checking into a hotel and going to Miss Marsh's house the next morning. But she had most likely received his telegram, and she and the children were doubtless awaiting him. So he hailed a carriage and proceeded to the Beacon Hill area. He expected the usual courteous greeting at the Marsh house. What he got was altogether unanticipated.

He rang the front doorbell several times, but there was no answer. He doubted that anyone had gone out on such a cold Sunday night. Perhaps the bell was not working, he thought, so he knocked—gently at first, then with force.

Finally, he heard the lock being turned. The door was pulled opened, and he saw the face of Kaki Kennon, Miss Marsh's Irish maid. Mark started to speak, but the look on Kaki's face stopped him. The young woman's cheeks were streaked with tears and her curly hair tumbled from beneath her white maid's cap. She was clearly in great distress.

"Oh, thank You, Lord. It's Professor Raymond!" she exclaimed.

"What's wrong, Kaki?" he demanded, thinking there must have been some accident. "My children—Miss Marsh—where are they?"

"You gotta do something!" Kaki screeched. "It ain't the girl's fault!"

She suddenly swung her arm out and pointed toward the closed parlor door.

Mark rushed inside the hallway, catching the sounds of raised voices coming from behind the parlor door.

"Go in, Professor!" Kaki urged. "Put a stop to it!"

Mark didn't hesitate. He dropped his travel case and raced to the parlor door, opening it upon a scene that made his blood run cold.

Gertrude Marsh was standing in front of the fireplace. In one hand, she held something that looked like a tennis racket. With the other hand, she was holding the arm of a wildly struggling Lulu.

Miss Marsh raised the thing in her hand as if to strike, but Max grabbed it and pulled it from his great-aunt's grasp.

25

Violet's Bumpy Ride

All the while, Lulu was screaming something about not being wrong, and Miss Marsh was yelling too.

"Stop!" Mark shouted. "Stop now!"

In an instant, he was between the woman and the girl. He had to pry Miss Marsh's fingers from Lulu's arm. Freed at last, Lulu ran to the far side of the room and huddled in a corner.

"What is happening here?" Mark demanded of his children's aunt.

Miss Marsh was so shocked at seeing the professor towering over her that she couldn't speak.

"Aunt Gert was gonna whip Lulu!" declared Max. "Aunt Gert wouldn't listen to us! She wouldn't hear the truth!"

As Max spoke, his Aunt Gert backed away from Mark and collapsed onto a chair. She immediately burst into great, blubbering sobs.

Max was breathing heavily, but his voice was calmer when he said, "Lulu did something, but it wasn't wrong 'cause she did it for good reasons. Really good reasons. But Aunt Gert wouldn't listen to her or me or Kaki. She just kept saying 'spare the rod, spoil the child,' and she was gonna whip Lulu with the rug beater."

He held up the strange implement so Mark could see it clearly. It was a wire contraption whose normal use was, indeed, to beat dirt from carpets.

Mark turned to find Lulu. She was still huddled against the wall, and though the corner where she stood was dark, Mark could see that she was trembling. He went to her and knelt down, wrapping his arms around her. She did not yield to his hug; her thin body remained rigid, though she continued to shake — with fear, the professor assumed. She didn't even look at him, but glared across the room at the fireplace.

"Lulu," Mark said softly. "It's me, Papa, and I'm here now. I'm here for you."

"I did it for Gracie," the little girl said in a hard tone. "And I'd do it again."

"Where is Gracie?" Mark said. He scanned the room quickly and felt alarmed not to see his youngest child.

"Upstairs in her bed, Papa," said Max, who'd come to his father's side.

"Will you go up, Max, and look in on her?" Mark said. "Don't disturb her if she's sleeping. But if this noise has awakened her, she may be frightened. Tell her that I'm here and will be with her soon. You stay with her until I come."

"I will, Papa," the boy replied. "I won't let her be scared."

"Good boy," Mark said with a warm smile. "Go on now."

Max went quickly, pleased that his father trusted him to care for his little sister. In truth, he was also glad to escape the parlor now that his father was in control. But as he mounted the stairs, he wondered why his Papa was in Boston. To Max, it seemed almost a miracle that his father had come just in the nick of time.

In the parlor, Mark led Lulu to a sofa and sat down beside her, putting his arm about her shoulders. He spoke very gently, though he was boiling inside at the evidence, before his very eyes, that Miss Marsh might violently beat any of his children.

"You're fine now, dearest," he soothed. "There will be no whipping, for I have put a stop to it. But I need to know what has caused such a commotion. You said that you did something for Gracie. Can you tell me what happened?"

Lulu said nothing. Her mouth was scrunched into a knot, and her eyes seemed blazing. Looking into her face, Mark realized suddenly that she was filled with anger, not fear, and that her stiffness and silence were acts of will.

He looked questioningly at Miss Marsh, whose sobbing had quieted. She merely slumped in the chair, looking crumpled and dazed and much older than she was.

Gazing about the room, Mark saw Kaki standing in the parlor door. She was wringing her hands, but she seemed in control of herself, so he asked her what had occurred.

Kaki glanced at Miss Marsh before replying. Then she said, "It's a kind of misunderstanding, sir. Miss Gert thinks Miss Lulu stole some food. At first, Miss Gert thought I took the food, and she was going to dismiss me, but Miss Lulu spoke up and said she done it. Miss Gert was so mad, sir. I never seen her so mad."

Then Miss Marsh spoke in a thin, exhausted voice, saying, "A thief must be punished."

Mark felt Lulu tense under his arm.

Kaki came forward and said in a rush, "Lulu's not a thief, sir. She took the food from the pantry, that's true. But it was for Gracie, mostly, and for Max. Maybe it was wrong to take it, but Lulu was that worried about her baby sister being so weak. I'd 'a done it me-self if I had the nerve."

Mark was confused now. "But why does Gracie need food? I've dined here many times, and Miss Marsh sets a fine table. How could the children lack proper food?"

At last, Lulu spoke up. "Aunt Gert is starving Gracie on corn mush and cabbage."

"What!" Mark exclaimed.

"It's a special diet, sir," Kaki hurried to explain. "Miss Marsh got it from one of her health books, and it's supposed

to be good for children. I can't see it me-self, but I'm not educated in modern ideas. Still, Gracie has been weaker, sir, since you was here at Christmas. Lulu was trying to help her sister, and Miss Marsh didn't understand that."

Mark was beginning to get a sense of what had taken place, but a great deal more explanation was required. He would have to get to the bottom of the quarrel, but he knew that no one was in a fit state to talk more on this night.

"I will be staying here," he said firmly.

"Yes, sir," Kaki said, and her relief was plain in her voice. "I'll take your case right on up to the guest room and get the fire lit."

"Thank you," Mark said. Then he stood and picked up Lulu, holding her close against his chest.

Her face softened, and she whispered, "You'll really stay with us, Papa?"

"I will," he said. "Now I'm going to take you to bed. I want you to get a good night's sleep, and we'll talk tomorrow."

Lulu laid her head against his shoulder and said, "Tomorrow, Papa."

As he was leaving the parlor, Mark said to his children's aunt, "Did you receive my telegram?"

Miss Marsh looked up at him with puzzlement and said, "Telegram? What telegram?"

So she did not know I was arriving, Mark thought. *Was it the Lord's intention that my telegram should go astray so that I might encounter the dreadful scene in the parlor? Is He leading me to question my assumptions about my children and their happiness? I believe He is giving me the chance to open my eyes and see. It is my job now to learn the truth.*

Kindly, he told Miss Marsh, "You and I will also talk tomorrow, Gertrude. Every story has many sides, and I want to hear yours. I promise that I will do you no injustice. The truth is more likely to be arrived at after we have all had a night's rest."

Mark took Lulu to her room, and Kaki came in a few minutes later. She would ready the child for bed, and Mark promised to return and kiss Lulu good night. Leaving Kaki in charge, he went to Gracie's room. He found Max sitting beside the bed and Gracie sleeping. Mark looked upon his youngest child, and the sight of her face, so completely free of care, was like a balm to his troubled mind. He gazed at her for some time and then leaned down to kiss her brow. Then he motioned to Max, and father and son left the room together.

Going to Max's room, Mark asked if his boy felt like talking. Max definitely wanted to talk. He wanted to tell his father everything, including his own role in Lulu's misdeed. But he also had a question.

"Papa, did you know about Aunt Gert's diets?" the boy asked.

"What diets?" Mark replied. "Can all this be about your great-aunt's kitchen?"

Max sat down on his bed, and Mark pulled a chair near.

"When you're here, Papa, we have regular food, so you don't see what it's like the rest of the time," Max began. Then he told all about Miss Marsh's odd ideas, including her latest fad for mush, cabbage, and bitter tea.

"It's okay for me and Lulu," Max said, "though we get pretty hungry. But it's not good for Gracie. She's never been real strong, but since you left after Christmas, she's gotten punier than ever. Sometimes she's so tired she can hardly stand up. I didn't know what to do, but Lulu did. She got the spare key to the food pantry on Saturday, and she took some meat and fruit and other things, and she gave some to me and some to Gracie. Then today, she took milk from the ice box for Gracie, and some fresh bread and butter, and Gracie ate them. But Aunt Gert noticed the missing food just before suppertime. She said that Kaki was stealing the food and would have to leave us. They were arguing, and we heard them, and Lulu ran in and said she'd done it. Aunt Gert just sent Lulu to her room at first. But I could tell Auntie was getting madder and madder. Me and Gracie had our supper and went to the parlor for our Bible lesson. That's what we do every Sunday. Aunt Gert was reading the Ten Commandments, and she got to 'You shall not steal,' and that's when she sent me to get Lulu. I thought she would just give Lulu a lecture, but she demanded that Lulu admit to being a thief and a sinner against God's commandments. Lulu wouldn't, and they were yelling something awful at each other. Then Aunt Gert got the carpet beater, and then you came in."

"Was Gracie present for all this?" the professor asked.

"No, sir. Aunt Gert had Kaki take her to bed when she sent me to get Lulu," Max said. "Auntie told me to go to bed too, but I didn't. I've never seen her mad like that before, and I was afraid for Lulu. Maybe Lulu did the wrong thing, but she did it for the right reasons. If she gets punished, I should too, 'cause I knew about it and didn't stop it."

"I don't think there will be any serious punishments," Mark said. Then he asked, "Has your great-aunt ever been cruel to you, my boy?"

Slowly, Max replied, "She tries to do what's right for us, but she has all these weird ideas, and she just doesn't know

anything about children. I've wondered about that, Papa, because she was a child. You'd think she'd remember what it was like. Do grown-up people just forget how they felt when they were young?"

Mark looked into his son's curious gray eyes. "Yes, they can, sometimes," he said ruefully. "It can happen because they had sad childhoods or were treated badly."

Mark paused. There was so much he wanted to ask Max, but he decided it was best to wait. At this moment, Max needed his father's assurances.

"Thank you for telling me all this. You've been of great help," Mark said. "We'll talk again tomorrow, after I've spoken with Lulu and your aunt. There will certainly be several versions of the story, and I believe that I will need your advice, son," he added with a wide smile.

"Really?" Max asked hopefully.

"Really and truly," Mark replied. He stood and reached to playfully tousle Max's thick, dusty blonde hair. Then he kissed the top of Max's head and said, "To bed now. Do you need any help?"

"Aw, I've been putting myself to bed for years, Papa," Max said. "A fellow my age doesn't need help like that."

Hiding a smile, Mark said, "Sorry, son. I should have known. Well, we'll have that talk tomorrow, just man to man."

Max, who was already pulling off his boots and stockings, looked up with a happy grin and said, "That'll be good, Papa. Just man to man."

In the Nick of Time

Mark looked in again on Gracie, who continued to sleep soundly. He noticed now that she did seem very thin, and he berated himself for not paying closer attention during his last visit. As he gazed at his little girl, he made up his mind. However good Miss Marsh's intentions might be, she was not a fit guardian for his children. His first duty was to remove Max, Lulu, and Gracie from this place as quickly as possible. The decision about moving to the South and taking the position at India Bay University would have to wait.

As he was contemplating his next actions, he heard sounds from the adjoining room. Gertrude Marsh was retiring for the night. He would deal with her in the morning.

He slipped from Gracie's room and went to Lulu's. Kaki was still there, and she was humming a lullaby when Mark entered. She put her finger to her lips, and Mark saw that Lulu was asleep.

He crossed to where Kaki was sitting and whispered, "I'll watch her now. You go on to your rest."

Kaki rose and replied in equally soft tones, "Thank you, sir. Your Lulu's a good girl, but she don't bend easy. There's a lot of stubborn courage in your daughter, Professor Raymond."

"We all have to bend at times," Mark said. "It's a lesson she needs to learn."

"That's true, sir, but if I can be so bold, I'd say this young one needs learning without breaking. She's got a will of iron, sir, and a heart for doing what's right. But I've seen iron snap like a twig when it ain't treated good. Once broke, it often can't be mended."

"That's good advice," Mark responded, and he was grateful for Kaki's observation. Her words reminded him again of how little he really knew Lulu and his other children. He, like Lulu, had much to learn.

With a curtsey, Kaki left, and Mark settled into the chair by Lulu's bed. He studied her as he had studied Gracie just minutes earlier. Her long, unruly blonde hair, pulled back from her face and bound in a thick braid, seemed almost white in the pale light from the oil lamp. But her cheeks were full of color, and he could make out the freckles on her nose. She looked healthy enough, but was she? She, too, was thin, though not as thin as Gracie. Lulu was a physically active child, and he'd attributed her wiry figure to her habit of running when others walked. Oh, why, he thought, had he been so quick to assume that everything was fine in Miss Marsh's household?

He shifted in his chair, and his mind drifted to India Bay and to Vi. He wished that she were with him. Vi would know what to do. She had an instinct—a gift—for understanding people that amazed him. She was only twenty years old, yet Vi was years beyond him in many ways. If she were here, she'd know what to do.

Lulu stirred, pushed at her covers, and mumbled something that Mark couldn't make out. Mark saw that she was frowning in her sleep, and thinking that his daughter was having a nightmare, he was tempted to wake her. But she settled again, and her frown vanished.

The fire in the grate was growing dimmer, and Mark felt the room becoming colder. He got up, and as quietly as he could, he added coals to the fire. Then he carefully adjusted Lulu's blankets. Seeing a knitted afghan on the foot of her bed, he wrapped it around himself and took his seat again. A warm bed awaited him in the guest room, but it didn't occur to him to leave. He wanted to be there when Lulu awoke.

 34

Watching his child sleep, he made a silent promise to her and to Max and Gracie. He would never again be a guest in their lives. Whatever trials they faced, from this moment forward they would be together—a family.

CHAPTER

Meanwhile

"For I know the plans I have for you," declares the LORD, "plans to prosper you and not to harm you, plans to give you hope and a future."

JEREMIAH 29:11

Meanwhile

*V*i Travilla had been dancing on air since she received Mark Raymond's telegram. She wasn't sure what to expect when she had been handed the wire at the telegraph office on the Monday after his last visit, but his words — "Courtship is the right word. Do you agree?" — had gone straight to her heart.

She had immediately sent a reply, addressing it to Mark in care of Miss Gertrude Marsh in Boston. It was a simple message: "Yes. Courtship is the right word. You are all in my prayers. Write soon. Vi."

She'd hoped for a letter within a few days, but more than a week passed before a thick envelope, addressed in Mark's now-familiar hand, was delivered. As soon as she was alone in her office, she ripped the envelope open, and after a brief search for her eyeglasses, she began to read. Mark's early correspondence to her had been written in a somewhat formal and reticent style. But this letter, sent from his home in Kingstown, brought the sound of his voice to her mind — his directness and his determination to weigh all aspects of a problem before making a judgment.

The first paragraph brought the news that Vi had longed to hear. With his children's eager agreement, Mark had accepted the offer to become head of the classics department at India Bay University, and he and his family would be moving to India Bay at the end of May.

Then he detailed all that had occurred since she last saw him — his arrival at Miss Marsh's home in Boston, the chaotic scene he'd encountered, and what he had learned about the care his children were receiving. Vi knew how much he must have struggled to control his temper as she read his description of what happened next:

> I talked with Lulu in the morning, and she forthrightly admitted taking the food. She was defiant and defensive, and even now she refuses to apologize to her aunt for her actions. We talked about why stealing is wrong. But I cannot in good conscience blame her as I would if she had done it for herself. I've imposed a small punishment—she must write a short essay about the meaning of the Eighth Commandment—and she is sitting across the room from me now, working on it.
>
> As for Miss Marsh, we also had a long conversation on the morning after the incident. I was prepared to upbraid her, but I had to hear her side of the story first. I questioned her closely about her discipline of the children. As she talked, I realized that Max and the maid, Kaki, were correct. Gertrude Marsh was doing what she thought best. The problem is that she does not think, not really. She is a lonely and silly woman who will follow any glib quack or charlatan into the most foolish of schemes. It emerged that strange diets and patent medicines are not her only eccentricity. She is also an ardent *student* of *philosophies* (her words) that are sheer balderdash. Her latest passion is for phrenology, which is the belief that one can read a person's character from the bumps on his skull! It might be comic if my children were not exposed to such nonsense. She has also invested a good deal of her money in fake business ventures, and I fear that a portion of the funds I have been sending

her for the children's care has been poured down the same drains.

In the end, however, I could only pity her. I told her that I was planning to move to the South and would take the children with me. She protested, but it was halfhearted, and I sensed that she is relieved to see her responsibility ended. I also advised her to consult a banker and lawyer before she made any further investments, but I doubt she will heed my words, for the woman's enthusiasm for anything "new" outweighs all ideas that are sensible.

I stayed only two days in Boston, just long enough to tell the children of my plans, pack what they would need for our journey back here to Kingstown, and arrange for the rest of their things to be sent. We are now all four in my apartment and cramped for space. But the children are so happy to be here that they do not mind tripping over one another. The woman who cleans for me is now also cooking for us, and my landlady watches over the children while I am teaching. I have taken all three children to my doctor, and he has pronounced Max and Lulu fit, if a little underweight. Gracie, however, has been greatly weakened by the poor food and lack of exercise. (It appears that Miss Marsh, by coddling Gracie, also did her the most harm.) Dr. Estevez is an old friend, and he kindly told me that I had "rescued" the children just in time. He was pleased to hear of our plans to move to the milder climate of India Bay, but he also warned me that Gracie may be vulnerable to illness for some time to come.

Violet's Bumpy Ride

Vi, I pray constantly that God will forgive me for my selfishness, and that I can make up for it with the children. I have come to understand that I must take full blame for this awful situation. I deliberately blinded myself to the truth. When I visited with my children, I failed to see what would be plain to any good parent. They pretended to be carefree for my sake, but if I had really looked into their eyes, I would have seen their unhappiness.

Vi stopped reading and removed her spectacles. There was a knot in her throat and tears in her eyes that blurred the words. *Oh, darling Mark*, she thought, *how hard it is for you to admit such things. I wish I could be with you this very minute, to hold your hand and try to make your pain more bearable.*

She sat for several moments, taking slow, deep breaths and blinking away her tears. When she felt calmer, she read on. If she had not been so sure of her feelings, Mark's next words might have shattered her. He wrote:

Dearest Vi, you must know now what kind of man I am. Arrogant, self-centered, vain, and as foolish in my ways as Gertrude Marsh. For the last four years, since their mother's death, my children have been made to suffer for my selfishness. I am determined to make amends, but I can never restore those years to them. All seems well right now, but who knows the extent of the damage I have caused?

Your telegram, which arrived just before we left Boston, brought me a sense of joy that I haven't felt for many years. Yet when I think of what I am asking you to take on, I almost wish that I had never spoken of my feelings. I cannot hold you to any promise made without your knowing of my unpardonable failures. We shall come to India Bay, for that is clearly the right move for the children. But it is a large town, and you need never contact me again.

What am I saying? I know you will not walk away from us, because it is not in you to abandon anyone. You will always be our friend. In a sense, you have been with me throughout this crisis, like an angel on my shoulder reminding me of what I must do. But how disappointed you must be—nearly as disappointed as I am in myself. The knowledge that I have harmed my children hurts me no less than the knowledge that I have surely destroyed your confidence in me.

I am sorry, Vi, for everything.

There was no closing to the letter—just his name: Mark. Vi turned back a page and read again the last few paragraphs.

"Now I should be crying," she said aloud, though there were no ears to hear her—except those of Jam, the mission's marmalade cat, who was sleeping on the windowsill.

"But I'm not crying," Vi went on to herself. "If anything, Mark Raymond, I am quite annoyed with you. Do you really believe that my affection is so shallow that it cannot weather a storm, or many storms? You're feeling guilty, and I know as well as anyone how guilt can color one's thinking. But this is no time to feel sorry for yourself or for me."

She put his letter to the side and got fresh paper and her pen from the desk drawer. Soon she was writing furiously, pouring her thoughts onto the pages.

Violet's Bumpy Ride

She'd been writing for almost an hour, and the floor was covered with crumpled sheets that she had revised and then rejected before finding the wording that exactly expressed her thoughts. She was reading over the final page of her letter when there was a rap at the door.

Mrs. O'Flaherty, Vi's dear friend and companion in the running of Samaritan House, entered to say that they were about to serve lunch for the students who attended the mission's elementary school. Mrs. O'Flaherty surveyed the floor of the little office, which looked as if it had been struck by a snowstorm. When Vi turned to her, Mrs. O'Flaherty let out a deep laugh.

"Have you decided to become a novelist?" she asked.

At Vi's quizzical expression, Mrs. O'Flaherty said, "I can see by the ink stain on your cheek and the blizzard of paper on the floor that you have been writing something of great import. I thought perhaps you'd decided to give up your mission work and become a writer like your cousin Molly Embury."

Vi stood and stretched her tired arms. "No, Cousin Molly's position as the family's only published author is safe," she said with a smile. "I have made a mess, haven't I?"

Vi stooped down and gathered up the wads of paper, disposing of them in a waste basket. Then she went to a small mirror that hung on the back of the office door.

Seeing the stain, she rubbed at her cheek with her handkerchief and managed to remove most of the inky black splotch.

"I received a long letter from Mark, and I was writing my reply," Vi explained.

Mrs. O' Flaherty asked, "Did he say anything about coming to India Bay? Has he seen his children?"

Vi turned to her friend. "His children are with him in Kingstown, and they will move here in late May. Mark has accepted the offer at India Bay University, and he says that the children are looking forward to the change," she said, her face glowing with delight. "I want you to read his letter, Mrs. O, all but the last two pages," she added, a flush spreading across her cheeks.

Vi took the letter from her desk and handed the bulk of the pages to her friend.

"Read it now," she said, motioning Mrs. O'Flaherty to the desk chair. "I'll supervise the children's lunch. Then perhaps we can discuss what he has written. I would like your opinion before I mail my response to him."

Vi was out of the door before Mrs. O'Flaherty could reply. Mrs. O smiled to herself as she watched Vi go. She thought about the changes she'd seen in her young friend in the past few weeks—the new energy and the renewed self-confidence. Vi would reach her twenty-first birthday in another few months, but age alone could not account for the maturity Mrs. O'Flaherty observed. And she was too wise to attribute all of Vi's growth to her love for the professor, though that was certainly a major factor.

The older woman believed that Vi had truly taken a leap forward and seized the opportunities that God had given her. Vi's faith in her Heavenly Father was never in question. But her faith in herself and her ability to overcome adversity had been less certain. Vi's strong sense of personal responsibility sometimes led her to doubt her abilities and to hide her worries for fear of burdening others. But their most recent confrontation with Tobias Clinch—the hotel owner whose hostility to their mission at Samaritan House had caused them so much trouble—seemed to have strengthened Vi's confidence.

Samaritan House had been in operation for less than six months, but in that short time, everyone who worked there had been altered by their experiences. To Mrs. O'Flaherty's mind, Vi had changed most of all. She'd grown from a girl with a fervent desire to serve the poor into a strong young woman who now understood in her heart that the true foundation of service is love—love *and courage*.

Turning to the professor's letter, Mrs. O'Flaherty put other thoughts aside. Mrs. O'Flaherty knew that the two pages Vi had kept to herself were personal. But what she read about the professor's visit to Boston and his concerns for his children revealed much about Mark Raymond's state of mind to the perceptive Mrs. O.

"Well, Vi girl," she said to herself as she folded the letter and laid it on the desk, "this looks like the greatest challenge yet for you. Are you ready for a husband and three stepchildren, if that is to be your future? Many young women would run away from such a tangle as this. But I don't believe you will, though I suspect that you are embarking upon a bumpy ride."

Mrs. O'Flaherty stood, and a sudden motion startled her. Jam leapt from the windowsill, scrambled behind the waste basket, and began batting at a ball of paper that had fallen onto the floor.

Mrs. O laughed at the cat and said, "Surprise me, will you? I have a feeling that our Lord has a number of surprises in store for us all in the near future. I wish I were as nimble as you, Jam, but in my faltering way, I will be here for Vi when she needs me."

She picked up Jam in her strong arms and lightly scratched the little cat's head, earning a satisfied purr in response.

"Max, Lulu, and Gracie Raymond," Mrs. O'Flaherty mused. "I wonder what they are like. I sense that at least one of them is a rebel at heart. Ah, well, we must wait until May to meet these young ones. And there is much work to be done right here at Samaritan House between now and then."

By the time Mark received Vi's letter, he and his children had made a good deal of progress. His apartment comprised the entire second floor of a large house on a quaint street several blocks from the prestigious Eastern university where he taught. The apartment included two bedrooms and a library as well as a small sitting room with dining space, a kitchen, and a new bathroom. Lulu and Gracie were now sharing one of the bedrooms, and Max was happily inhabiting the library, where his father had installed a sleeping cot.

On their arrival in Kingstown, the professor had tried to manage on his own for a couple of days. But he quickly realized that he was entirely unprepared for the day-to-day responsibilities of parenting three children. Clothing, feeding, educating, even entertaining? How did he go about it?

Mark turned to his landlady and the woman who cleaned for him. Seeing his desperation, his landlady, Mrs. Greeley, offered to mind the children while the professor was teaching his university classes, and the cleaning lady, Mrs. Tipton, would come each day except Sunday to prepare the children's lunch and also make dinner for the family.

47

Violet's Bumpy Ride

Mrs. Greeley was the widow of a university professor. She was both well educated and widely traveled, and she loved telling stories of the many trips she had taken with her husband. Mrs. Greeley's own children were grown and had families, but they lived in distant locations, so the lady rarely saw her grandchildren. She quite enjoyed "adopting" Max, Lulu, and Gracie for the time they would be in her home. She regretted the prospect of losing the professor as a tenant, but she knew that his new position at India Bay University was an excellent opportunity. And she, like Mark's physician, was certain that the warm Southern climate would be healthful for the children.

Mrs. Tipton was a no-nonsense kind of person who sized up the children's situation as soon as she met them. "Good food and exercise is what your young'uns need," she told the professor. "I'm not a fancy cook. Just good plain food and lots of it. Plenty of fresh air. And bowing our heads and saying thanks to our Lord for every day of living He gives us. Nourish their bodies and their spirits. That's how I raised my boys into the strong men they are today."

The professor could not fault her logic, and he was endlessly grateful to God for Mrs. Tipton's common sense and Mrs. Greeley's sincere interest in his children. Every day, Mark thanked his Merciful Father and resolved to learn everything he could from these two capable women.

Once the basic needs were attended to, Mark sought Mrs. Greeley's advice about schooling, and her suggestions were both practical and pleasing to the children. Mrs. Greeley herself would give lessons each day in reading, writing, and arithmetic. She would also work with them on American history (which had been her late husband's field of study), and the professor could hear their lessons every

night. That way, Mrs. Greeley counseled, Mark could evaluate their education to date and decide what kind of schools would be best for them after the move to India Bay.

Mrs. Greeley also volunteered to take the children to her church. She knew that Mark, though a believing Christian, was not a church-goer. She'd never criticized him for his preference, but she felt the children needed instruction in their faith, and Mark agreed. Max and Lulu had been sent to Sunday school in Boston, but their father was not sure how regularly. Nor did he entirely trust the Bible study that Miss Marsh had conducted in her Boston home. Who knew what odd interpretations of the Holy Word she had conveyed to his youngsters? He accepted Mrs. Greeley's offer, and he added it to the lengthening list of thoughtful acts for which he was grateful.

Barely two weeks after taking his children away from Boston, Mark was amazed to find that both he and they were living orderly lives and beginning to get to know one another. His son and daughters, he soon realized, had never blamed him for his years of negligence. It was their future happiness he must concentrate on now, not self-indulgent reminders of the past. He often thought of Vi and her ability to deal with a problem and then move beyond it. He wanted to be more like her — to learn from his mistakes so he would not be so likely to repeat them.

Mark's long letter to Vi had been written at a time when he was feeling deeply troubled about his ability to become a good father (or a good husband). He'd described to her all that had occurred in Boston, and in the end, he had put his doubts and regrets onto paper, hoping that she would not abandon him, but also determined to release her from any commitment she felt to him.

Violet's Bumpy Ride

Her return letter revived his hope. She chided him, gently but clearly, for doubting her faithfulness. And she told him that nothing he said or did could damage her affection. Vi's letter was not so long as his, but it was filled with such warmth and encouragement that Mark had to laugh at his own folly. He began to think that what he dreamed of might really come true—that Vi would become his wife and his partner in life and that his children would have this strong, wise, loyal, godly, and caring young woman as their mother.

✦

"It's fun hearing Papa's stories about India Bay," Gracie was saying to her sister.

The two girls were in their beds, enjoying the minutes of "talk time" their father allowed. It was a new routine for them. Their father would say bedtime prayers with his daughters and chat with them for a while; then he went to do the same with Max. The girls could talk together until Mark returned to their room, put out their light, and kissed them good night.

The young Raymonds were growing accustomed to many new routines, new people, and being in their father's life. Most important, all three children were discovering how much they truly *liked* their father. They had always loved and respected him, but because they saw him so little, he had been more of an ideal to them than a real person. Now, he was becoming their Papa who ate breakfast with them every morning, greeted them with hugs and kisses when he returned from his work every afternoon, listened to their lessons, asked about their activities, answered their questions, told them stories, heard their prayers, and tucked them in bed.

"I wish we could stay here forever," Lulu said to her little sister. "Being here in Kingstown makes me remember what it was like when Mamma was alive."

"Don't you want to move to India Bay?" Gracie asked. "It sounds very nice to me. Papa says it's warm in the South, and winter only lasts a few months."

"I want to be with Papa wherever he is," Lulu replied. "We're a family now, and I want us to stay that way. Just you and me and Max and Papa—and *nobody* else."

"We'll be together in India Bay," Gracie said happily. "And Papa says we'll have a big house and a big yard to play in. He said we might have a playhouse. Wouldn't that be fun, Lulu?"

"Oh, yes. A playhouse would be great fun," Lulu said with enthusiasm. "And I know Papa will find nice ladies to take care of us, like Mrs. Greeley and Mrs. Tipton."

"Maybe his friend—the lady with the flower name— will take care of us," Gracie suggested. "He talks about her a lot, so she must be nice."

"Miss Violet," Lulu said. "That's her name. She runs the house for poor people. And she's the lady who has the little girls Papa told us about—the two girls he helped when he went to South Carolina."

"Maybe those girls can be our friends," Gracie said, her voice growing drowsy. "I've never had any friends before, 'cept you and Max."

"That's 'cause Aunt Gert never let you out of her sight," Lulu said with the old indignation. "You can have friends now, Gracie, and everybody will like you."

Gracie didn't respond, and Lulu realized that her little sister was asleep. But something Gracie had said kept Lulu awake. When he spoke about India Bay, their Papa often mentioned "Miss Violet," as Gracie had noticed. And Lulu, who was alert to other people's feelings, sensed that this lady was somehow different. She didn't know why she felt this way, and she didn't know how to ask her father about it. She just felt that there was something different in her father's tone and his expression whenever he talked of "Miss Violet," and for some reason, it worried her. She forgot her concerns a minute later when Mark came quietly into the room.

"Still awake?" he inquired as he straightened the covers over Gracie.

"Yes, Papa, but I'm getting tired," Lulu said.

He came to her bed and leaned down to brush back a few frazzled strands of hair that had come loose from her braid. He continued to stroke her forehead gently, and his warm hand was so soothing that Lulu's eyelids closed. In a few moments, Mark knew from her soft, steady breathing that she was sleeping.

He kissed her cheek and said in a whisper, "God bless you and keep you, my dear."

Then he turned out the light and left the room. He still had several hours of work to do, but he didn't mind the late hours. The time he now spent with his children was precious to him, and he would not sacrifice a minute of it. He didn't want to miss even one of their smiles or their frowns.

As Mark went to his desk, where a stack of student papers waited to be graded, it dawned on him that something extraordinary was happening to him. Being with his children was changing his life. He knew in his heart that God had brought him to a crossroads on that cold night in

Boston. Without his usual weighing of facts and careful consideration of consequences, he had acted as a parent and protected his children. He had relied on his heart, and he had done what was right.

Now he was beginning to understand what being a parent meant. Children were God's gift, and raising them in God's way was both a privilege and a responsibility. He longed to bring them up in the training and instruction of the Lord.

In a very short time, Mark had begun to see the full meaning of every parent's responsibilities. And whenever he doubted himself, he turned to God. Not since his wife's death had he allowed himself to pray so openly and so personally. In his conversations with the Lord, the confident professor willingly became the humble student, and his Heavenly Teacher filled his heart with hope. After so many past mistakes, Mark Raymond was beginning to believe that, with God as his guide, he could become the earthly father that Max, Lulu, and Gracie deserved.

So Much to Be Done

Let us not become weary in doing good, for at the proper time we will reap a harvest if we do not give up.

GALATIANS 6:9

So Much to Be Done

*A*s winter changed to spring and the chilling cold gave way to sunshine and warming breezes, Vi's correspondence with the professor turned into a steady flow. He wrote long letters to her at least twice a week, and she responded with equally lengthy epistles. She wanted most of all to see Mark, but since that would not happen until the end of May, his letters were incredibly precious to her. She had heard people say that "absence makes the heart grow fonder." Now, the old expression had real meaning for her.

The postman who delivered the mail to Samaritan House noticed the flow of letters. Someone in the well-known Eastern university city of Kingstown was writing to Miss Violet Travilla every three or four days, and Miss Travilla was prompt with her own letters to the same distant location. The postman had heard some rumors about a romance for the young lady at the mission. So he suspected that the object of her affection might be her correspondent in the East. Fortunately, the postman was a man who kept his own counsel and didn't share his thoughts.

The residents of Samaritan House, however, had their own suspicions. They saw the bounce in Vi's walk and the cheerfulness she brought to every task, even the jobs that they knew she detested. At first, they attributed her mood to the success of their triumph over Mr. Clinch. Then several of the residents observed how Vi would retreat to her office every few days and emerge after a couple of hours with a thick envelope. The rest of the residents' correspondence was collected each day by Enoch Reeve, the mission's caretaker. But no one missed the fact that Vi always handed her "special" letters to the postman herself.

Mrs. O'Flaherty was the only person who knew the exact reason for Vi's behavior, but she said nothing and refused to be drawn into any discussions. She did, however, have a number of conversations with Vi, and in one of these, Mrs. O told her young friend just how curious everyone was.

"But why?" Vi asked. "I haven't talked of my feelings with anyone but you."

Mrs. O'Flaherty laughed warmly and said, "Oh, my dear, the happiness of love betrays itself like a light in a dark cave. It shines in your face and your footsteps. It beams in your enthusiasm for every mundane chore. Even Tansy, Marigold, and Polly have asked me about you."

"The girls?" Vi exclaimed. "Am I so obvious?"

"They don't suspect the cause, but they are happy to see you so happy," Mrs. O'Flaherty replied.

It was a late evening near the official beginning of spring, and Vi and Mrs. O were in the mission's combined dining and meeting room. Vi was setting one of the tables for the residents' breakfast the next morning, while her friend laid two other tables with the plates and utensils for the schoolchildren's lunch the next day. This was one of a number of productive routines they'd developed. Setting the tables in advance saved a great deal of time when the mission was busy during the day.

"There are many reasons for my happiness," Vi said with a charming laugh, "and not the least is my pleasure at having Tansy and Marigold back with us. They will soon be leaving us again, so I must make the most of their presence while we have them."

"It's not as if they will be that distant," Mrs. O'Flaherty said, "and we both know that living at Ion is for their own good."

Tansy and Marigold Evans, the orphaned sisters whom Vi and Mrs. O'Flaherty found and befriended on their first night at Samaritan House, had returned after a lengthy visit with their relatives in Pennsylvania. The young girls, raised in South Carolina, had never met their Northern grandparents and aunt, and it meant so much to discover that they had loving and caring family. But everyone, including the girls, realized that the elderly grandparents and aunt were not physically able to take two energetic children into their home. So it was decided that Tansy and Marigold would move to Ion, the Travilla family's large estate. Vi's mother, Elsie Dinsmore Travilla, who was now their legal guardian, would assume their care.

It was not an easy decision, but it had become clear that living at Samaritan House, which served primarily the white population of the poor Wildwood district, was not in the best interests of the two young Negro girls. As much as Vi abhorred the bigotry that separated white and black people, she had been convinced that Tansy and Marigold could all too easily be the targets of intolerance if they remained at the mission. At Ion, they would live with her mother and study with her youngest brother, Danny, and her sister Rosemary. They could make friends among the black and white children whose parents worked and lived at Ion. There would be no danger of the kind of ill treatment that was too real a possibility in Wildwood.

In fact, the girls had already made friends during several visits to Ion, and they'd become close to Ben and Crystal Johnson — Ion's house manager and head housekeeper. The couple had accompanied the children on their recent visit to Pennsylvania, and the Johnsons' loving kindness had been a key factor in the children's agreement to live at Ion.

The hardest part of the move was that Tansy and Marigold would be separated from Polly Appleton, the daughter of Samaritan House's much valued cook. The three youngsters had formed a strong bond almost at their first meeting, and it was going to be very hard on Polly to lose her friends. So Polly was near the top of Vi's list of priorities.

Vi kept an actual list on the back pages of her journal and consulted it every day. She checked off tasks that had been accomplished and added assignments that needed attention. To her bewilderment, the new additions to the list inevitably outnumbered the check marks.

Samaritan House was succeeding beyond all her expectations. Their afternoon meals—open to anyone in the community—now drew as many as fifty people a day, more when the weather was bad, and the number of people who stayed after the meals for Vi's Bible readings and devotion was growing. The home visiting, a service started in collaboration with several local churches during an epidemic of colds and fevers in January, brought meals to several dozen shut-ins every day. The clinic, run by Emily Clayton, was busy from morning to evening, and Dr. David Bowman now came two or three days a week to treat patients who needed a physician's care.

The school was perhaps the mission's most obvious success. Seth Fredericks, the young teacher whom Vi had engaged, had proved fully capable of transforming his first ragtag group of children into an eager band of students. Despite often difficult family circumstances, the children attended their new school with surprising regularity.

So Much to Be Done

Time and again, Vi found herself thanking God for the capable people who had chosen to devote themselves to Samaritan House. The mission had been her dream, but it was the people who made it real—beginning with Mrs. O'Flaherty, whose wisdom and steadfastness Vi relied on at every turn. Then there were Enoch Reeve and his wife, Christine, who had left their positions at Ion to become the mission's caretaker and housekeeper. This band of four adults, with the Reeves' baby, Jacob, were the first to take up residence in Samaritan House.

The Reeves lived in the converted carriage house behind the mission. Vi and Mrs. O'Flaherty (who was "Mrs. O" to everyone) had their private quarters on the mission's third floor, which they currently shared with the Evans girls and Alma Hansen, a young seamstress. A small set of rooms on the first floor was home to Mary and Polly Appleton. This group of people, plus Miss Clayton, Dr. Bowman, and Mr. Fredericks, had come together and shaped themselves into a family. In spite of their very different backgrounds, skills, interests, and ages, they were united by their faith, their respect for one another, and their mutual desire to spend their lives in helping others.

Over the past months, Vi had learned to trust the judgment of her fellow workers without reservation. Still, the residents did not always agree, and Vi was the chief decision-maker. What astonished her was that her friends, whom she regarded as so much wiser than she, accepted her leadership.

Violet's Bumpy Ride

Vi's list of priorities included many routine chores, such as ordering coal for the furnace and making inventories of their food supplies. Other tasks required more effort and greater planning if they were to go well.

One of these was the elevator. There had never before been an elevator installed in a house in India Bay. Mr. Archibald and his crew of carpenters had already begun constructing the two-story addition that would contain the machinery, and their work was attracting a great deal of attention. Some people in the neighborhood speculated about the safety of such newfangled machines, but most were intrigued by an invention that would enable people to rise effortlessly toward the sky.

Another new project began with the arrival of a very large object that now sat in a corner of the meeting room. It was a new, upright piano sent from a friend to Mrs. O'Flaherty. Mrs. O had written to her friend, the director of New York City's symphony, about her desire to teach music again. It was just a passing sentence or two, but it inspired the unexpected delivery of the piano a month later. Mrs. O was briefly overwhelmed with gratitude; then she quickly set about planning how best to use this gift to serve the people of Wildwood.

On still another front, Vi had made contact with Alma Hansen's brother, and a reunion of the siblings seemed likely to take place later in the upcoming months. In his letters to Alma, Rudy Hansen expressed his desire to leave California and join his sister in the South. Meanwhile Alma, a talented seamstress, was kept busy sewing for the mission and for her first client, Vi's sister Rosemary. She was also studying English with Mrs. O'Flaherty and making rapid progress. Vi naturally wanted to see Alma and Rudy settled comfortably

in India Bay, so on her own, she had begun making inquiries about employment for both Alma and Rudy.

Vi's efforts on behalf of Miss Bessie Moran were proving more difficult. Miss Moran had a boardinghouse not far from the mission. But her kitchen and laundry had burned to the ground in January, and now that gentle woman had lost most of her boarders because she was unable to provide the meals and cleaning that had attracted a good portion of her business. Vi had promised to find a solution, but her efforts so far had not been fruitful.

After Miss Moran's fire, Vi had learned a good deal about the dangers of fire in an area like Wildwood. Most of the houses and outbuildings were built of wood, and a spark from a stove or a dropped lantern could cause a raging conflagration almost before anyone noticed. The dilapidated houses stood very close together, so fires spread rapidly, and there was little to stop the devastation. Miss Moran had been fortunate to have her own well and cistern, for without water to drench the fire, her boardinghouse would certainly have been destroyed.

Vi decided that it was essential to get firefighting service in Wildwood. The leaders of India Bay had never been much interested in the fate of the people of its poorest district, but Vi could not see why Wildwood was any less deserving than other parts of the city. She'd already met several times with the mayor of India Bay. The mayor agreed that Wildwood had been neglected for too long, but he also made it clear that change would not come quickly or easily. He had spoken to her candidly about the pressures on the elected leaders of the city. From the richest citizen to the poorest, everyone wanted something from their government. With so many voices clamoring for

attention, the most powerful and influential would be the first to receive it.

Vi had come away from these meetings with a new understanding: just pointing out the problems in Wildwood would gain little. She would need a specific plan to solve the problems—one that would get the attention of the city fathers. Vi didn't have a plan and didn't know any other person who did.

Another notion that now preoccupied her was providing some kind of shelter—living quarters for people who had no homes. She often thought about Tansy and Marigold living on the streets when they were lost in Wildwood. Before Vi and Mrs. O'Flaherty discovered them, the girls had wandered the district, living on scraps of food and sleeping in the old mansion that was being converted into Samaritan House. But what of the other children Vi had seen lurking in the shadows of Wildwood's many alleyways? What of the people who lost their humble abodes when they didn't have money for rent? What of families driven into the streets by fires and floods?

The idea had come to her of establishing a refuge where those without roofs over their heads could find temporary lodgings. What was needed, Vi decided, was something like a hotel or a boardinghouse. She'd begun to look at empty properties in Wildwood, but the few buildings that might be suitable were occupied. She considered building a shelter, but were she and her friends ready for such a big project? Vi was acutely aware of the danger of trying to take on too much, so she prayed to her Heavenly Counselor for answers. Putting her problems, her worries, and her hopes in His hands, Vi trusted her Merciful Father to show her the way in His time.

When they first moved into Samaritan House, Vi and Mrs. O'Flaherty had driven to Ion each Sunday—attending services at the Travillas' country church and spending the day in the company of Vi's family. Since Christmas, however, the demands of Samaritan House had deprived Vi of these pleasant interludes. Whenever she went to Ion nowadays, she spent her visits closeted in business meetings with her mother and her big brother, Ed. To endure and continue its mission of service, Samaritan House had to be run like a business, and Vi was endlessly grateful to Elsie and Ed for their guidance.

Vi had known almost nothing about the day-to-day running of any kind of enterprise, though she had grown up observing her industrious mother. Elsie Dinsmore Travilla had long been involved in the management of Ion, the Travilla family plantation, and of her own large fortune—a most uncommon role for a woman of her generation. Vi knew that she had not inherited her mother's head for business, but she was doing her best to learn to be a faithful and wise manager.

Still, there were times when she felt nearly overwhelmed by the tasks of each day and her hopes for the future. The thought of Mark's impending move to India Bay kept her spirits high, but with the coming of spring, she found herself feeling unusually tired and sluggish.

Mrs. O'Flaherty noticed and, as she so often did, proposed a solution—that they take a weekend of rest and retreat at Ion.

"A whole weekend?" Vi said in surprise. "But I can't. There's so much to do here!"

Violet's Bumpy Ride

With a knowing look, Mrs. O'Flaherty said, "Samaritan House will not fall apart simply because you and I are away for three days. Vi dear, you have been in a near fever pitch of activity for months. You need rest before you wear yourself out. At Ion, you can be pampered for a few days and enjoy the company of your family. You can take walks, go for rides, or sit beside the lake and sketch. Do whatever *you* want to do. Body and spirit alike need rest and renewal."

The idea certainly appealed to Vi, but still she worried. What if there were an emergency of some sort? Her face was full of skepticism.

"Be guided by our Heavenly Father," Mrs. O'Flaherty went on in a firm tone. "You know His words in Isaiah 40: 29-31: 'He gives strength to the weary and increases the power of the weak. Even youths grow tired and weary, and young men stumble and fall; but those who hope in the LORD will renew their strength. They will soar on wings like eagles; they will run and not grow weary, they will walk and not be faint.' Young people always think that their strength is endless, but the Lord knows otherwise. In Matthew 11:28, He tells us, 'Come to me, all you who are weary and burdened, and I will give you rest.'

"I have another idea that might relieve your worries," Mrs. O'Flaherty went on persuasively. "We can take Tansy, Marigold, and Polly. Since Tansy and Marigold are moving to Ion next week, this will give them the chance to sleep in their new beds and grow accustomed to the house. A weekend at Ion should also reassure our young Polly. She can see where her two friends will be living and know that Tansy and Marigold will be safe and secure there. Rosemary and your brothers are looking forward to entertaining the girls, so you can have time to yourself."

This last remark made Vi smile broadly. "Why, this plan to visit Ion is no sudden idea of yours, Mrs. O!" she exclaimed. "I believe you have been in communication with Mamma, and the two of you have hatched this plot."

"I admit that I have consulted your mother," Mrs. O'Flaherty said, trying to keep a straight face. "She misses seeing you, Vi girl. Getting together to go over mission business is not a real visit for either of you."

"You're right, as usual," Vi sighed in resignation. Then she smiled again and said, "I concede to your greater wisdom, Mrs. O. A holiday at home. . .may I assume that you and Mamma have planned everything between you?"

"You may," Mrs. O'Flaherty responded. "All you need do is to pack your little case and be ready to depart after lunch on Friday. Ben is bringing the carriage to get us. We will return early on Monday, so you will not miss even one of those letters from the East that so brighten your life. Oh, I almost forgot. Emily will occupy your room while we are gone. I told her that we might be away, and she is quite eager to stay here."

"Does everyone know of your plot?" Vi inquired.

"Not everybody," Mrs. O smiled. "Naturally, I got Mary's permission for Polly to join us. But I thought that you would enjoy telling the girls."

"What would you have done if I had said 'no' to your proposal?" Vi asked with good humor.

"I didn't even consider the prospect," Mrs. O answered. "You can sometimes be stubborn, but your good sense generally triumphs. I prayed that the Lord would guide you to accept my 'plot,' as you call it, and He has answered my prayers."

"He answered mine when He first brought you into our lives," Vi replied. Affectionately, she placed her arm around

Mrs. O'Flaherty's waist and laid her head against her friend's shoulder for a few moments.

"I couldn't do any of this without you, Mrs. O," Vi said. "I wonder every day that you prefer life here at the mission to the excitement of New York and Paris and Rome. You could make your home anywhere."

Mrs. O'Flaherty returned Vi's hug and said, "Home is where the heart is, my girl, and my heart is here with you and Samaritan House."

The following Friday was warm and breezy, the winds of March having carried over into early April, and the sky was a pale blue, sprinkled with puffy white clouds. When Ben arrived at precisely two o'clock, Vi and her fellow travelers were waiting on the porch, enjoying the sunshine and the windy gusts that played with their skirts. Hearing the sound of horses' hooves, they looked up to see the large, closed carriage. To their surprise, a young lady with blonde curls stuck her head and arm out of one of the windows and waved gaily.

"It's Miss Zoe!" Marigold exclaimed with glee.

Ben maneuvered the large vehicle to a halt, and Zoe Love emerged. She was instantly surrounded by her friends, and Tansy asked her, "Are you going to Ion too?"

"I am," Zoe replied happily. "Vi's mother asked me to join your weekend party. It has been weeks since I've seen you girls, and I do believe that each of you has grown taller and prettier."

"We've missed you," Polly said, her voice soft but her eyes shining. "Have you been away somewhere?"

Zoe put her arms around all three girls and gathered them close. She said with a laugh, "I have been away in the world of books. You know that Vi's grandfather is my guardian and that I live with him and Mrs. Dinsmore. Well, Mr. Dinsmore is also my teacher, and he has had me studying very, very hard. Sometimes I am almost dizzy with all the new things I'm learning."

"I feel like that when we do arithmetic," Marigold said with a sympathetic nod of her head.

Mary Appleton and Christine Reeve, with baby Jacob on her hip, came out of the house to say farewell. Mary kissed Polly a number of times. This was the first time Mary had ever been separated from her six-year-old daughter for more than a day, and Vi saw that both mother and daughter were struggling not to shed any tears.

In just a matter of minutes, everyone was in the carriage. Ben cracked the reins, and with the three girls leaning out the side windows and waving, they were off on the journey to Ion.

Ben drove the heavy carriage very carefully, and the ride took longer than usual, but no one became bored. When they reached the open countryside, the girls were entranced by the landscape of spring—the greening trees, the bright yellow forsythia bushes and feathery redbud trees, the first crops of wildflowers that painted the earth in white and purple and yellow. They passed a barn that several young men were covering in a fresh coat of whitewash. They marveled at a recently plowed field where the wind was whipping up small, dusty whirlwinds that danced furiously for several seconds and then disappeared. They laughed with delight at a young calf gamboling near its placid mother in a small, fenced pasture.

Violet's Bumpy Ride

At one point Polly took in a huge breath of air and let it out with a long sigh. "I never smelled air like this," she said. "Never in my whole life."

Forgetting her usual reserve, Polly began asking questions. What made the grass turn green? Why were the flowers different colors? What do farmers do? How do cows make milk?

The women understood that Polly was a child of the city and answered her many queries as fully as possible. Zoe was especially attentive to the little girl, for she too had grown up in cities and only discovered the magic of these rural sights after she came to live in the South when she was sixteen. Zoe amused the girls greatly with a story of how she had learned to milk a cow.

Vi found herself smiling as she watched Polly. Vi had always been particularly observant of the passage of the seasons and sensitive to the rhythms of nature. But seeing Polly's eyes grow wide at the romping calf and the frenzied little whirlwinds, she thought how easily people, including herself, can take the beauty of God's magnificent creation for granted.

Mrs. O'Flaherty was also watching Polly. She touched Vi's arm and said in a low voice, "To see that child's wonder brings a passage of Shakespeare to my mind. It is a description of a young man, but somehow it seems to fit our little girl."

Then she quoted: " 'He capers, he dances, he has eyes of youth, he writes verses, he speaks holiday, he smells April and May.' "

"It does suit, except for the part about writing verses," Vi said, gazing at Polly.

"The young man in the play is in love, so Mr. Shakespeare's words are perhaps more apt for another person," Mrs. O'Flaherty commented wryly.

Zoe overheard part of this comment and looked up suddenly. "What young man is in love?" she asked.

"A character in Shakespeare's *The Merry Wives of Windsor*," Mrs. O'Flaherty replied.

"Oh, I see," Zoe said. Then she turned back to her conversation with the girls.

It was a very brief exchange, but Mrs. O'Flaherty had been struck by an odd note of sharpness in Zoe's tone. Vi had also heard the uncharacteristic stridency in Zoe's voice, and Vi was certain she knew its source. *My friend and my brother have not yet resolved their differences*, she thought, *and I begin to wonder if they ever will.*

A Weekend of Leisure

Therefore do not worry about tomorrow, for tomorrow will worry about itself.

MATTHEW 6:34

A Weekend of Leisure

$\mathcal{V}$i awoke on Saturday morning, and for a few moments she wasn't quite sure where she was. Then her head cleared, and she remembered—*I'm at home. I'm at Ion.*

Instead of jumping from her bed and hurrying to dress, as she did every morning at Samaritan House, she stretched lazily and stayed where she was. She thought of Mark Raymond, and her mind went back to their first meeting. It had happened here, in her own home. Every detail of that autumn day was crystal clear in her memory as she recalled her first impression of the tall, sandy-haired professor with the oddly attractive smile under his thick mustache. *How funny that I saw him as pompous and arrogant then. Now here I am counting down the days and the hours until I'll see him again.*

Her thoughts shifted to the previous evening. The family had dined on one of Crystal's very special suppers; then they'd all adjourned to the main parlor. Her mother had started the conversation by informing Vi that the twins, Harold and Herbert, planned to leave for the university in June, just a couple of weeks after their graduation from the Boys' Academy. Vi was surprised that her brothers would not spend their summer at Ion, but they were so obviously anticipating their new careers as "college men" that she was happy for them.

The talk had moved on to what Rosemary and Danny, the youngest of the Travilla children, were doing, and to Zoe's studies. Ed Travilla then gave Vi the latest news of the farm. Elsie updated her about other family members—especially her great-grandfather, Horace Dinsmore, Sr., whom Vi planned to see the next day—and read her the most recent letter from Missy, who was the oldest of the Travilla siblings and lived in Italy with her husband and young son.

In their turn, Vi and Mrs. O'Flaherty had answered everyone's questions about Samaritan House. Although Vi never tired of talking about the mission, she was glad that most of the evening's conversation had been focused on the rest of the family and their activities.

After more than an hour of catching up, they'd gathered about the piano. Mrs. O'Flaherty played and led them in rousing renditions of some new popular tunes. They'd ended the evening early, and Vi had gone to chat for a while with Aunt Chloe, the elderly nursemaid who had been like a rock of strength to the whole family for as long as Vi could remember. Then she'd said prayers with Tansy, Marigold, and Polly, who were happily ensconced in a bedroom next to Ben and Crystal's room.

Now, as Vi lay in her own bed and reviewed the events of the night before, she looked around her bedroom—the same room she'd occupied since she was five years old. The morning sun, filtered by the gauzy white curtains, poured in the two front windows, and the light yellow of the walls glowed warmly in the light.

Vi remembered when she'd been given this room. It had been so momentous to leave the room she had shared with Missy and to have her very own place. There had been some changes over the years. Her father had bought her the maple dressing table with its large oval mirror for her twelfth birthday. Her parents had replaced her small desk and chairs with larger pieces when she outgrew the originals. The stuffed armchair near the fireplace had been re-upholstered with a crisp chintz pattern of lilacs in shades of lavender, blue, and spring green. Vi smiled, remembering how her father would invariably complain that the seat was too low for his long legs whenever he sat in that armchair, took her on his lap, and read to her from her storybooks.

A fire burned in the fireplace. A servant had come in while she was sleeping, probably before dawn, to light it. This had always been done for her, but Vi suddenly felt a pang of emotion. Until she moved to Samaritan House, virtually everything that made her life so comfortable and secure had been done for her.

The clock on the mantel said that it was past seven, and Vi thought about how the wives and mothers of Wildwood would have been up for at least two hours by now. They would have gathered wood and lit their fires, fetched water, prepared breakfast, fed their families, dressed their children, and tidied their humble houses or rented rooms. Many would have already made their way across the city to their jobs as cooks and cleaners. Others were beginning another exhausting day at the textile mills and the laundries. There were no Saturday holidays for the working women of Wildwood. Fortunate was the family with a grandmother or an aunt who could watch over the children while their parents labored. But all too often, children as young as three and four were left to fend for themselves during the long hours when their mothers worked.

This last thought motivated Vi to rise quickly and dress. She rushed through her Bible reading, but her morning prayers were lengthier than usual. Her ruminations about the mothers and children of Wildwood had planted the seed of an idea, and she needed to talk it over with her Lord.

By the time Vi came downstairs and entered the dining room, everyone else was gathered at the table.

Violet's Bumpy Ride

"Good morning, sleepyhead," her brother Harold greeted her jovially.

His twin, Herbert, said, "I guess you don't have breakfast this late at Samaritan House."

"Never," Vi replied with a smile. "This is a luxury for Mrs. O'Flaherty and me."

She went to kiss her mother, and Elsie inquired if she had slept well.

"Too well, Mamma," Vi replied. "I might have lazed the whole morning away, for I'd nearly forgotten how good my old bed feels."

"Well, I'm glad you decided to get up. Your grandparents should be here soon to take you and Mrs. O'Flaherty to Roselands. Your great-grandfather is looking forward to seeing you, and the Conleys are most anxious for your visit."

Vi took her seat between Zoe and Danny, and Harold stood to give the blessing. Then the meal proceeded in a lively fashion. Vi asked her mother about Tansy, Marigold, and Polly. Elsie said that the girls had eaten earlier and Ben was taking them for a ride in the hay cart.

"I don't think you will see much of them this weekend," Elsie smiled. "Ben and Crystal have planned a full day: a picnic lunch with some of the girls Tansy and Marigold met during their last visit here and an afternoon visit with Miss Ellison at the schoolhouse. Tonight, they will dine with Aunt Chloe, and afterwards there will be square dancing in the servants' quarters."

Horace and Rose Dinsmore entered the dining room just as the morning meal was concluded. As the others scattered, Elsie, Vi, Mrs. O'Flaherty, and Ed remained at the table to chat with the Dinsmores.

"Will Zoe be coming with us to Roselands?" Rose asked Vi.

"She planned to, but the twins insisted that she go horseback riding with them," Vi explained. "They teased her into agreeing by telling her that she looked pale and weak—the effect, they said, of too much study with Grandpapa."

"If Zoe is pale, it is probably from too much socializing," Ed said in a disapproving way.

Rose smiled and said, "Zoe has made many good friends here, Ed. It is not unhealthy for her to spend time with others of her age. And I quite enjoy entertaining them at The Oaks. It takes me back to the days when your Aunt Rosie and Uncle Trip were Zoe's age and our house was always full of energetic young people."

"As I recall," Elsie said, "my little sister Rosie first met her dear husband at a spring dinner party that you and Papa hosted at The Oaks."

Elsie and her parents continued to reminisce for a few minutes. Vi listened, for she enjoyed hearing family stories. But she also saw that Ed was distracted. There was a scowl on his face, and Vi read in his dark eyes—so like her own—that he was caught up in some distant thought of his own.

When they finished their coffee, Ed excused himself, saying he had some chores down at the stable. This seemed a little odd to Vi because Ed was not dressed for stable work.

It immediately became apparent that she was not the only one who'd seen Ed's strange behavior.

"Is something troubling my grandson?" Horace asked Elsie after Ed had gone. "He seems moody of late. Do you think he is working too hard?"

Violet's Bumpy Ride

"He may have something on his mind, but I don't think it is related to his work," Elsie replied. "I'm sure he will sort it out. Now, the time has come for you all to be off to Roselands. Please give Grandpapa my love and tell him that I will come to see him next week."

Horace gave his daughter a kiss on her cheek. Then he turned to the other women and said in a cheery manner, "It's such a beautiful day that I brought the open carriage. Get your bonnets and shawls, ladies, and we'll be on our way."

Vi's visit with her great-grandfather was not lengthy. The senior Mr. Dinsmore had been quite ill for several years and was entirely bedridden. He quickly became tired, even when he was with the best of company. Still, he wanted to hear about Vi's work at Samaritan House.

"I'm proud of you, Violet," he said at last. His once booming voice was now thin and raspy, but his eyes shone as they must have in his youth.

"I rejected God many, many years ago," he went on. "I didn't live a godly life until I returned to His fold. I have His forgiveness, but still I regret those wasted years."

"Not wasted, Great-grandpapa, because they led you back to His love," Vi said.

"But all those years I was like a miser with my own love," the old man said. "That is why I am so proud of you—reaching out to others and spreading love instead of hoarding it up as I did. You are wiser at twenty than I was at sixty."

Vi didn't know how to respond. She loved her great-grandfather and hated to think that he might suffer from his regrets.

A Weekend of Leisure

Mr. Dinsmore didn't seem to notice her silence. With some effort, he raised his hand and gestured toward his dresser. His Bible lay there, and he said, "Read to me, please. I like the way you read."

Vi did as requested, selecting a chapter from the Gospel of Matthew. When she finished, she looked up and saw that her great-grandfather had fallen asleep, so she returned the Bible to its place and quietly left the room.

Downstairs, her grandparents, Mrs. O'Flaherty, and the Conleys were gathered in the front parlor.

"Mrs. O has just been telling us about your work at Samaritan House," said Cal Conley, the eldest of Aunt Louise's grown children and manager of Roselands. Cal was sitting in a straight-backed chair. His legs were crossed, and he balanced a rosy-cheeked little girl on one of his feet. Cal held her small hands and bobbed his foot up and down; the motion elicited excited cries of "Horsie! Horsie!" from the child.

Vi took a seat next to her cousin Virginia Conley Neuville, the mother of the laughing little girl, on one of the sofas. "It is so good to see you and little Betsy," Vi said. "She really is a beautiful little girl. She positively shines with health and cheer."

Virginia flushed at the compliment. "We've come a long way since you and my mother rescued us in New York," she said softly.

Her remark brought back memories of New York City's tenement-lined streets and the anxious day when Vi and Louise Conley had discovered Virginia and her infant daughter living alone in a dilapidated apartment building. Abandoned by her scoundrel husband, Virginia had struggled valiantly to sustain her baby, but her strength was nearly gone when she was found.

Violet's Bumpy Ride

"That's behind you now," Vi said, laying her hand lightly on Virginia's arm. "I must say that motherhood agrees with you," she added with a warm smile. "You look wonderful, Virginia. I've missed seeing you."

"No more than I miss having you close at hand," Virginia replied. "But from what Mrs. O has been telling us, the mission is progressing splendidly. I admit that I worried about how you might be received in Wildwood, yet Mrs. O says that the people there have welcomed your work."

"Most of them," Vi said wryly. "I believe we have overcome a lot of the initial suspicion, and we've made many friends in the community. There are still some who regard our services as a threat, but we haven't time to bother about them."

The others had turned their attention to Vi and Virginia, and they all joined in the conversation about Samaritan House. Vi was a bit surprised by the intense interest her aunt and cousins had in the operations of the mission. They asked many questions and also volunteered their assistance.

Cal, lifting little Betsy onto his lap, mentioned the delivery of firewood for distribution in Wildwood — one of the mission's first projects — and offered to organize a similar effort for the next winter. Hearing about Alma Hansen, Aunt Louise asked if the young seamstress might be able to take more clients for her dressmaking. Louise said that a couple of her friends were looking for a seamstress and could make good use of Alma's talents.

Then, as the visitors were preparing to leave, Virginia took Vi aside and said, "I've been thinking about the working mothers you described — how they must leave their children when they go to their jobs every day."

"What are you thinking about?" Vi asked with curiosity.

"Just that there are women all over this country who are seeking ways to help other women. I belong to a little club with some of my old friends. We meet every month in the city, and we talk a lot about what we can do for others. Most of my friends are well-off, married, and have children. But, my friends don't want to be ladies of leisure. They really want to do something, and I don't mean just donating large checks to their churches and charities. They want to work and be of service. Vi, may I tell my friends about Samaritan House and the needs of the people of Wildwood?"

"Please do," Vi answered. "Oh, yes, please do."

Vi put her arm around Virginia's waist and said, "I was praying this very morning for inspiration about the problem of the children of Wildwood. We have our school, but there is nothing for the small children whose parents work. Our staff at the mission is already stretched thinly, and I don't see how we can take on another challenge for some time. Yet I knew that our Lord would answer my prayer, and He has. It's you, dear cousin."

"I can't promise anything," Virginia said cautiously, "but these are good women with a real desire to contribute to our society. They may have some productive ideas."

Vi smiled, and her dimple signified her pleasure. "I think that 'productive' should be the watchword for this day," she said, "for our visit has produced good fruit. Whatever ideas you and your friends have are welcome."

"Well, hold us in your prayers," Virginia said, "and ask that God will inspire our thinking. 'He guides the humble in what is right and teaches them his way.'"

"That is from Psalm 25," Vi said. "I never heard you quote Scripture before."

Violet's Bumpy Ride

"I spend a good deal of time with my Bible now," Virginia said in a soft, sweet tone. "I look back at my years in New York, and I can see that, no matter how hopeless and alone I felt, God was leading me on a journey toward Him."

~

The party from Ion returned just in time for luncheon, and during the meal, everyone made plans for the afternoon. Horace and Rose, who were staying at Ion overnight, decided to read and perhaps take a nap before supper. Mrs. O'Flaherty wanted to visit with Aunt Chloe. Rosemary and Danny decided to go down to the schoolhouse in the servants' quarters and find Tansy, Marigold, and Polly. The twins planned to set up the croquet equipment on the side lawn and play the first game of the season, if Zoe would help them. She agreed, and even Ed said he would join them after he finished some necessary tasks.

The twins asked Vi to take part as well, but Elsie said, "I am hoping Vi might have a walk with me. I haven't been to the lake yet this spring, and I want to look at the dock. The winter was rather harsh, and the dock may need some repair."

Ed started to remind his mother that he had already inspected the dock, but he stopped himself before speaking. The dock was Elsie's excuse to be alone with Vi.

"If you are still playing when Mamma and I get back, I'd like a round of croquet," Vi told her brothers. "Perhaps Zoe and I might challenge you men to a game," she added with a twinkle in her eye.

Then she turned to Elsie and said, "I want to see the lake too, Mamma. I haven't been there since last autumn."

"I remember that day!" Rosemary piped up. "I was with you, and then Ed and Professor Raymond came to talk with us. Remember, Vi? The Professor made you so mad that you practically dragged me back to the house."

"I remember," Vi said in an even tone. Her voice was steady, but she could feel the heat of a flush spreading up her neck to her jaw and cheeks. *How could I ever forget that day?*

If anyone noticed Vi's reaction, they didn't comment. Elsie hurriedly excused her children from the table, and everyone went to their various activities. Vi fetched her mother's shawl, while Elsie consulted briefly with Crystal about the evening meal. Vi's Uncle Trip and Aunt Rosie and their spouses were invited for supper, so there would be a large number at the table that night.

The afternoon was pleasantly warm, and the air was filled with the sounds and smells of spring. Elsie and Vi walked across the lawn, which had not yet been mowed and was dotted with clumps of wild purple and white violets.

"They have come out just in time for your visit, my dear," Elsie said, bending down to pick one of the delicate flowers. "I've always had a special fondness for violets. As a child, I thought of them as little people who bloom with bright faces to greet the arrival of spring."

"Is that why you named me Violet?" Vi asked.

"You are named for your great-grandmother Stanhope," Elsie replied. "But I also liked the association with these charming flowers, and your Papa agreed."

"Mamma, I know the story about your first meeting Papa when you were a little girl. I know that it was many

years before you and he fell in love and married. But how did you and Papa know that you were right for each other?" Vi asked as they passed into the rough field that sloped down to the lake.

"Oh, my goodness, your question is nearly impossible to answer in words," Elsie said. "Love comes from the heart, not the head. Your Papa did not court me in the traditional fashion. In fact, his head told him that his love was impossible — that he was too old for me and that my father would not allow a marriage. And I? Well, I simply found myself loving him. I nearly made a terrible mistake, assuming that he was pledged to someone else. There was a great deal of confusion for a time, but from the moment when we finally told one another of our true feelings, there was never a doubt of our commitment."

"Did Grandpapa oppose your marriage?" Vi wondered.

"Not really," Elsie said. "He was concerned about the age difference. Edward was just two years younger than your Grandpapa, and they had been friends since boyhood. But when Papa saw our love, he raised no objection, though he did ask us to wait a year to marry."

Elsie laughed out loud and said, "To me, the year of our engagement was the longest of my life. I thought it would never end."

Vi didn't say anything else, and they walked on for several minutes until the lake came in view between a break in the trees that surrounded it.

Vi and Elsie stopped to take in the scene, and while they were gazing down at the silvery gray, rippling water, Elsie said, "I shall not ask you and the professor to wait as long as your father and I did."

Vi was astounded. She turned to stare at her mother, who was still looking toward the lake.

"H—how—how—?"

"How do I know?" Elsie said, completing Vi's question. "I've been in love myself, and I have observed its effect on many others. Believe me, darling, the signs are unmistakable."

Elsie now looked into her daughter's deep, dark eyes and smiled brilliantly.

"From what I see in your lovely face, Vi dear, may I take it that Professor Raymond shares your feelings?" Elsie inquired.

At last able to muster a reply, Vi said, "He does, Mamma! He has asked my permission to pay court, though I don't know how it can be a conventional courtship."

Taking her daughter's hand, Elsie said, "I understand. You both have obligations to others. . . your work at the mission, and Mark's children, whom you will soon come to know. In fact, you and Mark still have much to learn about one another. I just want you to know this—whatever decision you and Mark make about your future, I support you. I love you. I know you've prayed about your decision. I am also extremely fond of Mark and would welcome him as a son-in-law. Should you and he pledge to become one in marriage, my heart will be with you both. I give you both my full blessing."

Vi felt tears springing to her eyes, and she almost fell into her mother's open arms.

"Thank you, Mamma!" she exclaimed as Elsie embraced her. "Thank you so very much. I was hoping for the chance this weekend to tell you all about—about everything. But you already knew my heart. Oh, Mamma, you are the best, most understanding mother any girl could have!"

Violet's Bumpy Ride

Elsie stroked Vi's hair and said, "It's time we both stop thinking of you as a girl. You are a grown young woman who will soon celebrate her twenty-first birthday. And she is facing one of the most important decisions of her life."

Elsie's voice softened as her words became a prayer: "Dear Father in Heaven, thank You for blessing me with a daughter such as my Violet—so strong in faith and so willing to give of herself to others. Be with her, Lord, and with Mark as they embark on this journey together. She knows that the road may not be easy and that their final decision will profoundly affect others beyond themselves. Make them strong, Father, and help them to be wise. If it is Your will, let their love for each other grow and encompass the three Raymond children and bring them together as a family. Our hope is in You, and we trust You to lead us always. Please, Lord, comfort Vi and Mark through whatever trials may lie ahead, and if their future is to be together, bless their union with Your love."

Vi held on to her mother for several minutes. Then she stepped back, and taking a handkerchief from her pocket, she dabbed at her eyes.

"Mamma, have you ever noticed that tears of joy do not sting like the other kind?" she said with an embarrassed smile. "Yet they are just as wet."

Elsie put out her hand and lifted Vi's chin. "Your Grandmother Rose taught me never to be ashamed of my tears, whatever their cause. Now, tell me how Mark's plans for the move are progressing."

Vi was happy to share everything she knew with her mother. Most important, Mark had made arrangements to rent a house—one of those he saw on his last visit to India Bay. Vi confessed that she had driven past the house a number of times and understood his choice. It was a charming

older dwelling not far from India Bay University, and it offered a spacious garden.

Vi continued with the news that Mark had also found a cook—a young Irish woman named Kaki Kennon, who had worked for his children's aunt in Boston.

"She wrote to Mark that she had been dismissed by the aunt," Vi said. "She didn't say anything critical of her former employer, but Mark is sure that the dismissal is the result of the dreadful scene he walked in on at the aunt's house. The young woman stood up for Lulu that night, and he was impressed by Miss Kennon's courage and her kindness. His children are very fond of her, so he offered her the job. Miss Kennon will come to India Bay early in May to ready the house, and I've invited her to stay with us at the mission. Mark has asked me to help him find a housekeeper."

"I can give you several names," Elsie said, "and I'm sure Mrs. Lansing will know more women for the position."

"I will be grateful for your help, but I have an idea I'd like to explore first," Vi responded with a sly smile. "If it works, it will solve several problems."

Vi then shared more good news. Mark had applied for Max to attend the Boys' Academy, and Max had been accepted. Vi had sent him information about several possible schools for Lulu and Gracie, and he was interested in one in particular.

"Miss Broadbent's Female Academy?" Elsie guessed.

"Yes. How did you guess?" Vi asked.

"Because Susan Broadbent is one of the most gifted educators I know," Elsie explained. "Her rigorous curriculum includes instruction in science and Latin and Greek, and I feel sure that appeals to the professor."

Vi smiled and said, "It does, Mamma. He expects no less for his daughters than his son."

"Only God knows the future, but He expects us all—women as well as men—to prepare for whatever may lie ahead," Elsie said thoughtfully.

They had reached the lake. After a quick look at the dock, which needed a few planks replaced but no major repairs, they strolled along the water's edge to the boathouse. They talked further of the Raymonds and then of Tansy and Marigold's approaching move to Ion.

Turning back toward the house, they fell into a comfortable silence—just mother and daughter happy to be together. But as they started back up the hill, Vi asked, "Is there any way that one can prepare to be a stepmother?"

"No more than one can prepare to be a mother, I suppose," Elsie said.

Then she stopped still and said, "Wait a moment, Vi. I spoke too quickly and without thinking. I have never been a stepmother, so I cannot really answer your question. But I know who can—your Grandmother Rose. I was nine when she and your grandfather married. I loved Rose very much, but I know that stepping into the role of mother to me was not easy. You should talk with her."

"Does Grandmamma Rose know about my feelings for Mark?" Vi asked.

With a smile, Elsie said, "It's not something we have discussed, dearest. But your grandmother is a very perceptive woman. I do not believe she will be surprised to hear about the cause of the twinkle in your eyes and the glow in your face. Yes, you should talk with her about your concerns."

Vi looked at her mother with serious eyes. "I haven't wanted to admit it to myself," she said, "but I do worry about my ability to be what Mark's children need. I am so anxious to know them, and I'm sure I will love them. But that's not enough to be a good mother to them, is it?"

"Perhaps not, but love is the foundation," Elsie mused. "God is love, and our Savior taught us that all things are possible with Him. Remember that, my darling—*all* things are possible with Him. I wish I could assure you that everything will go smoothly, but as a mother myself, I know it won't. I think your grandmother can alert you to some of the pitfalls that lie ahead of any stepparent. My advice is to trust God to guide your every step and do not doubt the power of your love for Mark and his little ones, and God's love for all of you."

"I'll try not to," Vi said as they walked on up the hill to the house.

"Love can move mountains," Elsie responded. "Begin with love, and I have faith that you will be able to move three young hearts."

When Elsie and Vi reached the house, they saw Harold and Herbert knocking croquet balls about the side lawn in an aimless fashion.

"Are you ready for our game?" Vi asked. "Boys versus girls?"

"It will have to be you against the two of us," Harold said in a peevish way.

"But where are Zoe and Ed?" Elsie wondered aloud.

"Who knows?" Herbert replied in a tone that conveyed his frustration. "We were all playing, and Ed said something joking to Zoe. He didn't mean any harm, but Zoe got

as red as a radish and ran off to the house. Then Ed got mad and stormed off toward the stable. They're as bad as an old married couple."

"What do you know about old married couples?" Harold laughed.

Herbert grinned and said, "Not a thing, but that's what people say when a man and a woman like each other but can't seem to get along."

"Do you remember what Ed said?" Elsie asked without any sign of humor.

"Something about a fellow we all know," Harold replied. "Charlie Haynes—the one everyone calls 'Fog' because he seems so dim."

"Charlie Haynes is a really nice person," Vi said in protest. "Just because he doesn't care about sports and horses—that doesn't make him dim. I've always thought him very smart and interesting, if you take the time to know him."

"Well, Zoe thinks so too, and that's what she said," Harold went on. "Then Ed made a joke about 'old Fog.' I didn't hear his exact words, but whatever he said, he sure riled Zoe."

Vi was thinking how hard Zoe had been working to be patient and not let herself become angry with Ed. So whatever her brother had said, Vi knew that it must have been genuinely provoking. At the same time, she doubted that Ed intended to annoy Zoe.

"I wish those two would admit how they feel about each other and get over all this silly fighting," Herbert said.

"What do you mean?" Elsie asked her son.

Herbert blushed and lowered his head. "It's pretty obvious, Mamma," he said bashfully. "We all know that Ed and Zoe are sweet on each other."

"We know," Harold said, "but maybe Ed and Zoe don't."

Elsie spoke up, trying to make her voice stern. "It isn't for us to speculate, boys. Now that Vi is back, I imagine she can convince Zoe to rejoin your game. And I trust you will be perfect gentlemen," she added with a warning look.

"We won't say a thing, Mamma," Harold answered, knowing exactly what his mother meant.

"Not a word," Herbert agreed.

Elsie turned to go inside, and Vi caught up to her.

"Who was it who called jealousy 'the green-eyed monster'?" Elsie inquired.

"It was Shakespeare in his play *Othello*," said Vi.

"Of course," Elsie sighed. "Shakespeare — so attuned to the peculiar ways of the human heart."

"Do you think Ed is jealous of Charlie Haynes?" Vi asked.

"I think he has heard that Charlie Haynes is the most recent young man of our acquaintance to admire our dear Zoe," Elsie said. "I think Ed is finding rivals where there are none."

They didn't see Ed again until supper, and by then, both his and Zoe's moods were much improved. Trip and Eloise Dinsmore arrived, then Rosie and her husband, and everyone was in excellent spirits. The evening progressed without any more unpleasant incidents, and Vi found herself settling back into family life with ease. While Samaritan House was always in her thoughts, she allowed herself to relax and enjoy her brief holiday from work.

Violet's Bumpy Ride

On Sunday, she had an opportunity to speak privately with her grandmother, and Rose was delighted to hear about Vi's new relationship with Mark Raymond. Rose gladly told her granddaughter about her own experience as a stepmother, sharing memories about herself and Elsie that went back more than forty years.

When asked for her wisdom, Rose said, "Each situation is so different that I cannot tell you exactly what to do, but I will venture one piece of advice. Do not worry about being a stepmother yet. What the professor's three children need, I imagine, is a friend. That is what happened with Elsie and me. We were friends from the first. Our love as mother and daughter grew from that friendship—and our mutual love for your grandfather. My point, Vi dear, is that children need understanding adults in their lives just as they need friends their own age. Give yourself time to get to know the professor's three young ones as individuals. Treat them as I see you treat the Evans girls and little Polly."

"What if they do not accept me?" Vi said, asking the one question that haunted her. She had never voiced her worry to anyone before, yet it was the one possibility that, she knew, could end her hopes. She could not marry Mark if her presence in his life might damage his relationship with his children.

"Is there any reason they would not?" Rose asked.

"I don't think so," Vi replied thoughtfully. "But their lives have been difficult since their mother died, and their reunion with Mark is so new. They may resent me."

"Yes, they may, at first," Rose said frankly. "And you should be alert to such feelings on the children's part. But do not be afraid, Vi dear. And do not try to bear any problems on your shoulders alone. If you and the professor are to become partners in this life, you must share your trials as well as your triumphs — together and with our Lord."

Then Rose laughed in her lovely way and added, "My advice for you today is not to go putting your cart before your horse. It is one thing to be prepared for problems that may arise. It is quite another to expect troubles where none may exist.

"The words of Isaiah 42 offer a beautiful promise for you to keep in mind. 'I will lead the blind by ways they have not known, along unfamiliar paths I will guide them; I will turn the darkness into light before them and make the rough places smooth. These are the things I will do; I will not forsake them.'"

6

Packing
for a Move

*Therefore, prepare your
minds for action. . . .*

1 PETER 1:13

Packing for a Move

*T*he Raymond family now had less than a month left before their move from Kingstown to India Bay, and their packing was already underway. At least, Mark was boxing up his extensive library and his papers, and his children were doing their best to help.

Mrs. Greeley was also at work on new clothes for Lulu and Gracie. The kindly landlady was making some items herself, and she had also engaged a local seamstress who was busily turning out dresses suitable for the Southern summer ahead. Mrs. Greeley had been shocked by the state of Gracie's wardrobe. The little girl had many lovely things, for Miss Marsh had showered the youngest Raymond with beautiful clothing. Yet to Mrs. Greeley's experienced eye, very little in Gracie's collection of frilly, lacy outfits was suitable for a child who needed to run and play and enjoy the freedoms of childhood.

Lulu, who had decidedly not been pampered by her Boston aunt, had a more serviceable wardrobe than Gracie's. But she needed new clothes because she had gained some weight since coming to Kingstown—her thin frame becoming more robust with a healthy diet and exercise—and most of her old clothing was now too tight for her.

Max had also grown stronger and taller, and his father undertook the task of acquiring new clothes for him. Father and son had had an important talk, and together they agreed that there would be no more short pants in Max's closet.

"Do my new dresses look too plain?" Gracie asked Lulu one afternoon as they played in their room. Lulu was helping

her little sister cut out dresses for the paper dolls that were among Gracie's favorite playthings.

"Your new dresses are really pretty," Lulu said firmly. "They're a lot more comfortable than those frilly dresses that Aunt Gert made you wear, aren't they?"

"Oh, yes," Gracie said. "I feel real good in my new clothes. I like having pinafores. I just thought maybe…"

She hesitated, and Lulu said, "You're going to look like a real girl now. Aunt Gert dressed you up like a fancy doll, but you're not a doll. You're a real girl."

"I know that," Gracie giggled.

They continued cutting out paper dresses for a while; then Gracie asked another question: "Do you think there'll be lots of children to play with in India Bay?"

"Papa says so," Lulu said. "He says there are families with children in just about every house on the street where we're going to live. He says that's why he rented the house, so we'd have children to play with."

Lulu set her scissors down and said in a wistful way, "I sort of had some friends at school when we were in Boston. But Aunt Gert never let other children come into her house, so I never got to know those girls very well. I'd like to know some girls my age. I'd like to invite friends over to play and have fun."

"Me, too," Gracie agreed. "Papa told me that Miss Violet has a brother and sister just a little older than you and Max. Maybe they can be your friends. I can't wait to meet Miss Violet and her family. They sound like such nice people."

I can wait, Lulu thought to herself in a spiteful way. She had never asked her father about "Miss Violet," but his frequent references to the young lady in India Bay had caused Lulu's vague disquiet to become real anxiety. She worried that this woman might be more than a friend to her father. In her mind, Lulu began to form a picture of "Miss Violet"—a vision concocted from images gleaned from reading countless stories about innocent children made to suffer by cruel stepparents.

The three Raymond children loved to read, and both Lulu and Max had a fondness for the adventure stories sold at the newspaper stands. The stories were printed like little magazines, on cheap paper, and could be purchased for a penny. Max's favorites were tales about cowboys in the Wild West and pirates sailing the seven seas. Lulu preferred stories about people in peril, especially characters who were children like herself. The more frightening the danger, the better the story, as far as Lulu was concerned.

Miss Marsh would probably have denied the children such reading matter if she had known they were buying it. But their Aunt Gert had paid so little attention to Lulu and Max—aside from seeing that their chores were done and punishing them when a task did not met her standards— that she hadn't bothered to notice what they were reading.

Their father, however, had taken notice. Mark didn't want to forbid their reading; instead, he was encouraging Max and Lulu to enjoy adventures that were much better written. He had introduced them to the American novels of James Fenimore Cooper and Nathaniel Hawthorne and the fantastic stories of the French writer Jules Verne. In just the past week, Mark had received a copy of Robert Louis Stevenson's *Treasure Island* from a friend in England, and he and the children were reading it aloud—a chapter every night before bed.

Lulu decided for herself that books like *Treasure Island* were much more exciting than any penny magazine story,

largely because good writers made the people in their stories seem more real. But her earlier reading still influenced her thinking, and her mental picture of "Miss Violet" grew more threatening by the day.

I bet most people think she's very pretty, Lulu told herself as she continued to cut out the paper clothing for Gracie. *I bet she's short and plump and has green eyes like a cat. And she has red hair and long fingernails, like a witch, and she smells like rotten apples. She doesn't do any real work at that mission, but she makes all the poor people work for her. Only Papa doesn't know about that because the poor people are afraid to say anything against her. But he'll find out how mean she is when we move to India Bay, and he won't like Miss Violet anymore.*

Lulu smiled to herself. She liked this story. She had other versions. In one of them, "Miss Violet" was very old, about forty, and very greedy and cunning. In another, the lady was tall and beautiful but cold and heartless, like Snow White's wicked stepmother.

In her heart, Lulu knew that none of her fantasies could be real, for her wise and kind father could not be friends with the kind of women Lulu imagined. She couldn't explain, even to herself, what made her so hateful about "Miss Violet." But she did know that it was wrong to judge someone she didn't know, so Lulu didn't share her thoughts with Gracie or Max, for doing so would surely make her brother and sister think less of her.

Why do I always see things so differently? she wondered to herself. *I wish I could be more like Max and Gracie and think the best of people, but I can't. I guess Aunt Gert was right about me, and I'm just bad. But I don't feel bad for thinking the way I do about that "Miss Violet." If I'm right about her, she could ruin everything for Papa and us.*

Gracie interrupted these ruminations with a question that surprised Lulu. Gracie was dressing one of the paper dolls in a wedding dress when she asked, "Do you think Papa will ever get married again?"

"Never!" Lulu exclaimed, though this was her own secret worry.

"Papa is happy with our family just the way it is," Lulu went on, raising her voice in a way that made Gracie stare at her. "He loved our Mamma so very, very much. You've heard him say that there could never be anyone like her. No, no, a thousand times no! He won't do that to us!"

Gracie turned her soft blue eyes back to the paper doll, and Lulu didn't see the wistful expression on her sister's delicate face.

Several moments passed before anything else was said. Then without looking at Lulu, Gracie spoke in her quiet way.

"I'd like to have a nice stepmother," the little girl said. "Somebody like Mrs. Greeley, only young and pretty like our Mamma was."

Not wanting to upset her sister, Lulu struggled to lower her voice as she replied, "I don't think there are any nice stepmothers, and nobody could ever be as sweet as our Mamma. Besides, we can make Papa happy by ourselves now that we're all together. He tells us every day how happy he is to have us with him."

"But—" Gracie began. Lulu cut her off.

"Don't even think about it," Lulu said firmly. "We're a family, Gracie. We don't need anyone else. Especially not some selfish old stepmother who wants to take Papa away from us."

Gracie didn't say any more, but she had suddenly lost interest in the paper dolls and began to put them away. She

didn't like it when Lulu got mad. She decided that maybe Lulu was right. In their fairy stories, stepmothers were cruel people, so maybe Lulu was right. But that idea made Gracie sad. She was so young when her mother died that she had no real memories of her own. All she knew of her Mamma came from the stories that Lulu and Max told her. She wanted so much to believe that someday she would have another loving mother to care for her and be her friend. But if Lulu was right, that would never happen.

As the day of the move drew nearer, Mark began to think of himself as a man caught up in a ceaseless hurricane. Between his work at the university and making the arrangements for the move, he barely had a moment to catch his breath. Still, he didn't allow anything to interfere with the time he devoted to his children. Nor did he fail to keep up his correspondence with Vi. Each letter he received from her seemed to fill him with a fresh burst of energy. No matter how hectic, every day brought him closer to being with his beloved Vi again.

Mark was pleased to see how much Max, Lulu, and Gracie wanted to help him with the many tasks necessitated by the move. They didn't complain as the apartment was transformed from a comfortable dwelling to something resembling a warehouse stacked with wooden crates and barrels filled with their belongings.

Even Mark hadn't realized how many books he owned until they began to pack his collection.

"What are all these books about?" Gracie asked her father one afternoon as all four Raymonds worked at emptying

Packing for a Move

Mark's library shelves. Mark was on a ladder, handing books down to his son. Then Lulu and Gracie would carefully dust each book before Max put it into a packing crate.

"They're about everything I know and all the things I want to learn," Mark said.

"Papa, have you read every one of these books?" Lulu asked.

Mark laughed and said, "No, dearest, not all of them by any means. Some of them are meant to be read from cover to cover, like your adventure stories. Others I use for my research. There is information in those books that helps me with my studies. Then there are books I use for my classes. They are written in the languages I teach."

Max wanted to know how many languages his father could speak.

"Well, the two languages I teach — ancient Latin and Greek — I cannot speak," Mark said. "At least I cannot speak them as the people did many centuries ago. We think we know how they would have sounded in ancient times, but we cannot be sure. I also understand some Aramaic, which was the language of Mesopotamia."

"Mrs. Greeley says that Latin is called a 'dead language,' because there isn't a country where people use it anymore," Max informed them.

"That's right," Mark agreed. "Latin was the language of the Romans and their empire. But today, Rome is only a city in the country of Italy, and the people there speak Italian."

"Then why does anybody care about Latin?" Lulu questioned. "If nobody can speak it, why should we learn it?"

"That is a very reasonable question, Lulu," Mark said. Then he went on to explain how the use of Latin had died

out after the fall of the Roman Empire, but how the old language influenced and mixed with new languages. He explained that Latin was still used in science and in the law and how a form of ancient Latin was spoken in the Catholic Church. He talked about his own work, translating ancient texts into English so people could read what people had written long, long ago. And he told them how the Bible had first been written down in Hebrew and Aramaic and Greek and how it had been passed down over time and translated into other languages, like Latin.

Lulu didn't understand everything her father was saying, but she found herself listening with great interest. She was learning some Latin and Greek from both her father and Mrs. Greeley, but until now, she'd thought it very dull and boring. Hearing her Papa talk about his work, she had her first inkling of why, for him, learning about the past was an adventure even more exciting than the stories she read, because it was real. For him, languages that people hadn't spoken in a thousand years were like the buried riches in *Treasure Island*. Except that her father didn't care about gold coins.

Mark went on to tell the children how his work as a scholar of ancient languages had led to his interest in exploring ancient civilizations. He said that everything — even the tiniest bead or bit of broken pottery — unearthed in places like Troy and Egypt was a clue to lives of the people of the past. Then he told them about what he would be doing in Mexico in the summer. The children knew that after their move to India Bay, their Papa would be going away for six weeks on an expedition.

"So if you can find out what kind of houses people had and what foods they ate, that helps you know what their lives were like. Is that how it works, Papa?" Max asked.

Packing for a Move

"We can never know exactly what life was like for people in the past," Mark replied, "but we can begin to put together a picture and increase our understanding."

"Is it fun for you?" Gracie asked.

Mark laughed. "Yes, it is. It is fun for me," he said. "Now, I wouldn't say that to my fellow professors at the University, for we are supposed to be very, very serious about our work. But I can confide to my children that it is also fun for me."

He climbed down from the ladder and lifted Gracie up from her seat on the floor, holding her in one of his strong arms.

"What makes me happiest of all is being with you three," he said. "I love my work, but it is nothing compared to the love I feel for you. Why, look what happiness you have given me today. You should be complaining about all the stress and strain of packing up my dusty books, but instead you've given me the fun of telling you about dead languages and digging for clues to the past. How God has blessed me! To have three such curious and thoughtful children."

He held out his free arm, and Lulu and Max came to his side to be enfolded in a warm hug.

"Papa, when I'm older, can I go with you on one of your adventures?" Lulu asked. Her imagination had left behind all thoughts of cruel stepmothers and children in peril. She was envisioning herself accompanying her father across desert sands and through thick jungles in search of hidden cities and buried treasures.

"I'd like that," Mark said. "But we need not wait till you are older. In just a few weeks, the four of us will embark on an adventure in the South. Think of it, children. We will be going to a place unlike any place we have ever lived, and

we'll meet people we've never met before. We're all Americans, but in the South, they do many things a little differently from what we are accustomed to, and we shall have to study their ways."

Setting Gracie down, Mark added with a smile, "You might say that we will be archaeologists of the present. We have a great deal to learn when we get to India Bay."

While his father was speaking, Max's expression had turned quizzical.

"When I was at school in Boston, we learned that the South was a bad place because the white people there made the black people their slaves and treated them cruelly," Max said. "Is that true, Papa?"

"Yes, son, it is," Mark replied solemnly. He sat down on one of the book crates, and the children gathered around him.

"Millions of black people in the South were forced to be slaves," Mark began to explain. "It was a cruel and heartless system that lasted for more than two hundred years, until we fought the Civil War to free the slaves and unite the country."

"What's a civil war?" Gracie asked.

"It's a war fought by people who live inside the same country," Mark said. "In our country, the soldiers of the North fought against the soldiers of the South for four years, until the Southern armies surrendered."

"Were you a soldier, Papa?" Lulu asked, thinking how handsome her father would look in a military uniform with a shining saber at his side.

"I am not *that* old, my dear," Mark responded with a wry smile. "The American Civil War began almost twenty-five years ago, when I was about the age you are now. My father fought for the North, in a Massachusetts regiment. He was badly wounded at the battle of Gettysburg, and he died of his injuries not long after he returned home to us."

"I never heard that before!" exclaimed Max, his eyes round with wonderment.

"I have never talked much about it," Mark said, "but your grandfather was a fine Christian man with a strong sense of honor. You should know about him, and all your grandparents. I have been badly remiss in not telling you of your own family history."

Lulu's mouth had puckered into a pout as she listened to her father, and now she said in a hard tone, "You should hate the South, Papa. You should hate the people there because they killed your papa. We should hate all the people down there, shouldn't we? They're our enemies, aren't they?"

"Hate?" Mark said with surprise. "No, Lulu, for how can we hate anyone when Jesus teaches us to love everyone? We have His commandment in the book of Matthew. Do you remember it?"

Lulu said nothing, so Max spoke up. "I know, Papa," he said. "It's Jesus' words in Chapter 5." Max quoted, " 'You have heard that it was said, "Love your neighbor and hate your enemy." But I tell you: Love your enemies and pray for those who persecute you, that you may be sons of your Father in heaven.' "

"Very good, Max," said Mark.

Then he looked at Lulu and continued, "The North and South fought a bloody war because both sides thought they were right. But that war is over, and now we are one people again. It's true that some people still hold hard feelings, and we should pray to God that their hearts will be healed by

His love. But the people of the South are not our enemies, Lulu, and we are not their enemies. The people of India Bay will welcome my children into their homes and their hearts just as they have welcomed me. I want you all to be open to this new adventure we are about to start. Do you think we can follow our Lord's way and make this move in a spirit of love and hopefulness? Can we be good neighbors and friends to the people of India Bay?"

"Sure, Papa," Max said with confidence. "The war was bad, but it would be wrong to hold it against anybody now."

"I'm 'cited about moving," Gracie agreed, as she pulled at her father's coat sleeve to get his attention. "I want to love everybody in India Bay."

"I know you do, darling," Mark said, hugging his youngest child warmly.

"Does your friend Miss Violet have any slaves?" Lulu asked in a pert tone that, fortunately, her father didn't seem to notice.

"Miss Violet never owned slaves, though her parents and grandparents did," Mark answered honestly. "I know that everyone in their family regrets that fact, and they do everything they can to make amends for their transgression."

"Tell us more about Miss Violet's family, please, Papa," Gracie requested.

"Yes, Papa. How do you know them?" asked Max.

Mark welcomed Gracie's and Max's questions, for he wanted his children to be interested in the people who, he hoped, would become as family to them before very long. He decided to tell them about Ed Travilla and how they had met at the University. He talked while he and the children returned to their packing, and the time went by quickly as

he told his youngsters about Ed and the other Travilla children and their large farm outside India Bay.

Lulu listened closely and even asked a few questions of her own. She didn't like to admit it, but the Travillas did sound like nice people. She was growing curious about them, and in spite of herself, she wanted to meet them. But when Mark mentioned "Miss Violet" again, she heard something in his voice that made her heart ice over. She lost track of what her father was saying, becoming wholly caught up in her own defiant thoughts.

I'll go to India Bay and make lots of friends with girls and boys like me. Maybe I'll even be friends with those Travillas, because that would make Papa happy, ran the words in her head. *But I don't care what the Bible says. I won't be friends with that old "Miss Violet." Not in a million, billion years. Not ever!*

7

Cleaning Up

What is the way to the abode of light?

JOB 38:19

Cleaning Up

Kaki Kennon came to India Bay two weeks before the Raymonds. Her responsibility was to prepare for the professor and his children, and she was eager to see his house and determine what needed to be done. Mrs. O'Flaherty and Enoch met the young Irishwoman at the railway station and took her straight to Samaritan House, where she would be staying. Kaki could have spent the day resting from her long train trip, but she was not the kind of person to let grass grow under her feet. So within two hours of her arrival in India Bay, Kaki paid her first visit to College Street, accompanied by Vi and Mrs. O'Flaherty.

" 'Tis a nice big place," Kaki said approvingly, as Vi drove the buggy into the driveway of the white-painted dwelling. "But this yard could use some tending. Professor Raymond said for me to hire on a gardener if need be."

Indeed, the lawn was overgrown, and the bushes that outlined the front of the house were in need of trimming. In the flower beds, weeds were battling with the late spring flowers, and here and there about the grounds, mounds of dead leaves from several large maple trees added to the appearance of neglect.

"From what we've been told," said Vi, "this house has been empty for more than a year."

"It has the look of a rascally boy who needs a good haircut, a bath, and a set of clean clothes," Kaki laughed. "But I'll soon have it set to rights."

They'd reached the front door, which was centered on a wide, wood-floored porch that ran the entire length of the

front of the house. Kaki took a ring of keys from her bag. She fumbled for a few minutes, trying different keys, and Vi felt her own anticipation rising. Vi had driven past the house a number of times, and on one occasion, she had ventured onto the property to walk about the garden and peek in the windows. But she had not been inside, and she was enormously curious about the house Mark had selected.

"There!" Kaki exclaimed as one of the keys slipped into the lock and turned with ease.

The three women entered and looked around. Outside, the day was clear and sunny, so the darkness inside made Vi blink until her eyes adjusted to the lack of light.

They were standing in a spacious entry that opened into rooms on the left and the right. A stairway climbed one wall of the entry. The rooms were entirely bare of furniture, but heavy draperies covered all the windows (as Vi had discovered that day when she'd tried to get a glimpse of the interior).

Kaki sniffed noisily and said, "It smells dusty but not musty. That's good. I wouldn't want the professor findin' his home reeking of damp."

Mrs. O'Flaherty went into one of the rooms. "Let's open these drapes and get a real look," she said.

Vi and Kaki hurried to draw back the curtains in the other room. Sunlight flooded in, and Vi instantly knew what had attracted Mark to this house. The light revealed that both front rooms were large and well-proportioned, each with a fireplace and polished wooden floors that, even under a coating of dust, reflected the light.

"I'd guess this is the living room," Mrs. O'Flaherty said of the room to the right.

"This one's for dining," Kaki called from the opposite room. "There's a china cupboard on one wall."

Cleaning Up

"Oh, it's lovely," Vi said softly.

Kaki had come to where Vi stood. "Sure, and it will be lovelier when it's cleaned. There's more for us to see, though."

More there was, and each room they entered confirmed their initial impressions. They went from room to room, opening the drapes. In spite of the dust and cobwebs, the house appeared to be in very good condition. Kaki and Mrs. O'Flaherty were both pleased by the kitchen, which included both an old-fashioned wood-burning stove and an almost new gas stove. At the rear, they found an extension that had been added to the original house. It was shaped like the letter L and included another porch, two airy rooms with fireplaces, and a bathroom. Kaki concluded, rightly, that one of the rooms would be hers, and she liked that it was so convenient to the kitchen.

Vi discovered a sitting room behind the living room. The sitting room, though not large, was equipped with shelves from floor to ceiling along one wall, and she immediately thought what a wonderful library it would be for Mark.

Upstairs, there were five rooms and a bathing room. As Vi toured the space, she was thinking how Mark's three children could each have a bedroom of their own. She smiled to herself, imagining these empty rooms ringing with the sound of children's voices.

In the meantime, Kaki had found a small door that opened on rough stairs to a low attic. Ever practical, Kaki searched for signs of water leaks and other damage, but the light here was too dim for her to see much. In her head, she made a checklist of possible problems—the gas lighting, the coal furnace, the water supply—in addition to any leaks.

Violet's Bumpy Ride

Returning to Vi and Mrs. O'Flaherty, Kaki expressed her concerns. Vi suggested that Mr. Archibald, the carpenter, might be willing to visit the house and give it a thorough inspection.

"Oh, that would be settling to my mind," Kaki said with a sigh of relief.

"Mr. Archibald will be at Samaritan House tomorrow morning," Mrs. O said. "He's coming to give our new elevator one last test before we put it in use. You can talk to him then."

"An elevator?" Kaki asked. "Whatever do you need with such a contraption?"

"It's for the people who have difficulty walking up the stairs to our clinic," Vi said with some pride. "Our elevator will make it much easier for them."

"Well, that's a good thing, I suppose," Kaki said, her tone conveying doubt.

She'd seen elevators in the warehouse district in Boston, but she wasn't at all convinced that they were safe for ordinary humans like herself.

Kaki and Mrs. O'Flaherty began to discuss pressing matters, such as how much help Kaki would need for the cleaning and how to find a gardener. But Vi soon drifted away and took one more turn around the house. She looked more closely at each room, noticing this time how simple yet elegant the design was. She observed the details—the finely carved moldings, the unobtrusive gaslights with their beautifully etched glass lanterns, the oversized windows like those at Ion. Mostly, she enjoyed the lightness of the house. Standing alone in a large upstairs bedroom, Vi was conscious of how the sunlight was filtered by the green trees outside so that it flickered gently over the pale-colored walls and the ceilings. Vi imagined how bright the rooms would be even in the dull days of winter.

The light is almost magical, she thought to herself. *It seems to dance with pure joy. Mark has told me about his apartment in Kingstown and Miss Marsh's townhouse in Boston. He has described them both as darkly paneled and Miss Marsh's house as drab and dreary. I'm sure it was the light that drew him to this house. I remember when he looked at houses with the real estate agent. It was a cold January day, but the sun was shining. I'm sure Mark came here and pulled back the drapes, just as we did today.*

She smiled unconsciously, picturing Mark striding through these very rooms and throwing wide the curtains. *I know he saw more beautiful houses, yet he chose this one. Perhaps here, he sensed how much his life and his children's lives were about to change after their years of sadness and separation. Perhaps he knew that he was about to take a new and more perfect path, guided out of his darkness by the light of our Lord.*

" 'You are my lamp, O LORD,' " Vi said aloud, quoting from David's song in Second Samuel, " 'the LORD turns my darkness into light.' "

"If it's God's will," Vi went on as if Mark were really there with her, "I shall accompany you on your new road and walk by your side until death do us part. And when our journey in this world is ended, we will be together forever in His Heaven."

Her voice echoed slightly in the empty room, and her own words came back to her — "in His Heaven."

In a bare whisper, she said, "Thank You, dear Lord, for Your endless gift of love. Please, Heavenly Father, watch over Mark and his children as they make their way here, and keep them safe. Be a lamp for their feet and a light for their path.

Violet's Bumpy Ride

And bless this house, which will soon be their home, with Your love and Your peace."

Vi's heart was so full that she dared not stir a muscle, lest she lose the feeling. But a voice from downstairs roused her. It was Mrs. O'Flaherty, calling out that it was time to leave. Reminded of her duties back at Samaritan House, Vi hurried to the bedroom door and replied that she was coming. But she couldn't resist lingering for one more look around the light-filled room.

The next two weeks were busier than any Vi had experienced at the mission. On top of her work at Samaritan House, she made at least one trip to the College Street house every day. Whether these visits were absolutely necessary was doubtful, but Vi took such obvious pleasure in the transformation of the house that none of the mission residents questioned her frequent absences.

Charmed by Kaki's Irish ways, Mr. Archibald had agreed to inspect the professor's house from top to bottom. The very next day, he spent almost four hours there and brought back a good report: the house was solid as a rock, the roof was in excellent condition, and there were no leaks. He recommended that the chimneys, the coal-fired furnace, and the gutters be cleaned, but he said these were just precautions.

While Mr. Archibald was crawling about the attic and foundations on College Street, Kaki and Mrs. O'Flaherty went shopping for all the necessary household tools and managed to hire two reliable girls from Wildwood to help Kaki with the housework. At the suggestion of the local

butcher, they also engaged his elder son to do the necessary outdoor work.

Early on the second morning after Kaki's arrival in India Bay, she and Enoch set out in the mission's cart. The cart was piled high with mops, brooms, and other cleaning essentials, a couple of ladders, a table and some chairs that Enoch had brought down from the mission's attic, and a large basket of food prepared by Mary Appleton.

Vi and Mrs. O'Flaherty followed the cart in the buggy. There were two passengers in the narrow back seat — sturdy, brown-haired girls who looked as alike as twins. They were the Hudson sisters, Sarie and Teenie, whom Kaki had employed. Sarie was seventeen, and her sister a year younger. They said little during the ride, but their excitement was obvious in their bright grins and the way they playfully poked one another and pointed to people and buildings along the way. The girls rarely had a chance to leave the confines of Wildwood, so all the sights of a normal weekday in the busy city were an adventure for them.

On entering the house on College Street, Kaki immediately took charge. She would help Enoch unload the cart, while the Hudson girls were to begin taking down all the curtains in every room. "Them moth-eaten old drapes ain't good for anything but stoking a fire," Kaki pronounced. "We need 'em out of here before we do any washing and dusting."

Vi and Mrs. O'Flaherty said they would begin cleaning the kitchen, which surprised and pleased Kaki. She hadn't expected the elegant young lady and her friend to get their hands dirty with such menial work. Kaki accepted their offer with gratitude, but decided to keep a cautious eye on their work.

121

Violet's Bumpy Ride

Kaki had never supervised others before, but Vi soon realized that the young maid had a natural gift for leadership. Kaki organized the chores and gave instructions in a clear, firm manner. But her directions were laced with the humor of someone who enjoys the work she is doing and wants it done well. The sisters, who were the youngest of six Hudson children, also understood the meaning of work, and they made every effort to carry out Kaki's instructions to perfection.

As the work progressed, Vi saw that Mark had made an excellent choice when he employed Kaki Kennon. His house would be run with efficiency and good cheer. Still, Mark and his children would need a housekeeper, and he had entrusted Vi to find someone. Vi already had an idea of who might be best for that job. She had waited to meet Kaki before putting her idea into action; she knew how important it was for the two women to be congenial. After a few days getting to know Kaki, Vi was convinced that her idea was sound, and she went to visit Miss Bessie Moran.

Miss Moran had been struggling to make ends meet since the fire at her boardinghouse. She had lost most of her boarders, and those who remained seemed likely to depart soon. Miss Moran was a kind woman and quite clever in many ways. But she had no head for business and was having little success at attracting new lodgers.

When Vi spoke to Miss Moran about the possibility of becoming the Raymonds' housekeeper, the older lady's face lit up with the first untroubled smile Vi had seen since the fire.

"Work for Professor Raymond?" Miss Moran said in a chipper tone. "Why, I would be honored, if he really wants me."

"You remember him?" Vi asked.

"I do. Very well. I'll never forget when you and he came to my door with those baskets of food on the day after the fire. He was so nice to help. One doesn't expect strangers to be so nice. And he's handsome, too," she added with a wink.

"Did you know that he sent me a check?" Miss Moran then inquired.

"He did?" Vi asked in amazement.

"He wrote the nicest note and included a check. He said I was to spend the money for whatever I needed, and I can tell you, Miss Violet, I put it to good use. I bought food for my boarders and a warm jacket for Jimmy Farmer. He was the one who raised the alarm about the fire, you know. I might have lost the house if that boy hadn't summoned the other men so fast. And the poor child's coat was just ruined with the smoke and water. It was very generous of the professor to send me that money."

"It was," Vi agreed. "And it was equally generous of you to use his gift to benefit others."

This remark caused Miss Moran to blush with embarrassment, and Vi thought how much younger the good lady looked when she was happy.

They talked more about what Miss Moran's duties would be if she became the professor's housekeeper and about the responsibility of caring for his three children.

"I like looking after young ones," Miss Moran said a little shyly. "When I was a girl, I wanted to grow up to be a governess. I thought what a good life it could be, to care for children and be their teacher. But I'm not well educated like you, Miss Violet. I had to leave school when the war started."

Violet's Bumpy Ride

The conversation soon turned to living arrangements. Vi spoke about the comfortable rooms in the College Street house and said that Miss Moran could live there if she wished.

"But what about my house?" Miss Moran asked in an anxious tone. "It was my parents' home, built back when Wildwood was a fashionable neighborhood. I could sell it, I suppose. Mr. Clinch has made offers on several occasions. But I couldn't bear to see my house turned into a hotel or something worse. My family lost everything except this house during the war. It's silly, but keeping the place has been like keeping their memory alive."

"I have an idea about that," Vi said with a reassuring smile. "Let me tell you what I have been thinking. I know we can find a solution if we put our heads together."

When Vi left Miss Moran's house an hour later, there was a particularly sprightly spring in her step. It was a beautiful May day, and despite the poverty of the neighborhood, Wildwood was blooming. Walking back to the mission, she saw several of her neighbors, and she stopped to chat with each one. Mrs. Peters was setting out some flower seedlings around the foot of her rickety front steps. At the Widow Amos's little house, her grandson was yanking weeds from a patch of ground where the widow would plant her summer vegetables.

Mr. Yarborough, a veteran who had lost most of his sight in the war, was sitting in a chair in his yard. "Howdeedo, Miss Violet?" he said when she greeted him. "Don't this sunshine feel good? Can you smell that new grass? I surely do like it when May finally gets here."

"Will you be coming to the clinic this week?" Vi asked.

"Yes, miss," the man replied in a cheerful manner. "Even if I didn't need to see the doc, I'd come by for the company."

Cleaning Up

Vi said good-bye and continued on her way. Suddenly, a verse from one of Mrs. O'Flaherty's favorite ballads darted into her head:

There are twelve months in all the year,
As I hear many men say,
But the merriest month in all the year
Is the merry month of May.

She was still humming the old tune when she got back to the mission. She was anxious to go to her office and begin a letter to Mark — a letter that would be brimming with good tidings. But she took time to have some pleasant words with all the people who had come to Samaritan House that day.

"What's got Miss Violet so happy?" whispered a man to a young mother who was sitting beside him on a bench outside the mission clinic.

"Maybe she got some good news," the mother speculated.

"Musta been right good news," the man said with a chuckle. "Her feet are barely touchin' the floor."

Twelve days later, Vi could hardly believe all that had been accomplished. Every nook and cranny of Mark Raymond's house was clean and sparkling. The old drapes had been replaced by new ones made by Alma Hansen, and she had chosen fabrics that allowed the light in every window. The gas had been turned on, so at night the house took on a golden glow.

Violet's Bumpy Ride

Mark had shipped most of his furniture and his many crates of books from Kingstown, and though there were not nearly enough pieces to fill the house, Vi and Kaki made certain that his things were placed in the most comfortable and inviting way. They had added some items brought from Ion, including carpets and beds for the upstairs rooms.

Vi personally put Mark's books on the tall shelves in the sitting room. She knew that he would re-arrange his library to suit his needs, but she did the work anyway, reading every title and finding comfort in the mere touch of the leather bindings. She noticed which books seemed to be most used—the ones with well-worn covers and turned-down pages—and these she placed on the lower shelves so that Mark could find them easily. It took almost two full days to complete the task, and Vi's legs and arms ached from climbing the ladder again and again, carrying heavy volumes to the top shelves. But it was a labor of love, and she laughed away the pain.

The outside of the house looked as inviting as the inside. The butcher's son, a strapping twenty-year-old named Elwood Hogg, had raked, mowed, weeded, clipped, and pruned every square foot of the lawn and garden. The house's wooden exterior needed only a few minor repairs, but with Enoch's help, Elwood cleaned all the gutters and gave the window shutters and trim a fresh coat of paint.

When Kaki surveyed all this work, she rewarded Elwood with praise. "When I saw this place, I said it was like a ragtag boy needing a haircut and a clean suit of clothes. Well, you've dressed him up fine, Elwood. My, oh my, it be a pretty house! With them bushes cut back, you can see how white and shiny it is. I'm gonna like living here. And the professor'll be real happy. I just know he will."

Cleaning Up

But what had been happening at the mission while so much attention was being given to College Street? Vi hadn't been so distracted as to forget her duties, though the other mission workers had gladly filled in when she was away. She certainly didn't miss the anticipated day when the new elevator was put into service.

Vi hadn't planned for the day to turn into a special event, but a number of Wildwood's residents knew what was going to happen and gathered at the mission early on the morning of the elevator's "launching."

Vi, Dr. Bowman, and Emily Clayton took the first official ride up to the clinic and down again. After their ride, Vi asked if anyone in the small crowd would like to go up. There was an animated buzzing among the people, but no one volunteered. Vi prevailed on Mr. Archibald, who was supervising the proceedings and beaming with pride, to explain how the elevator worked. He wisely kept his remarks brief. But he emphasized the strength of the construction and the safety of the machinery.

Vi then asked again if someone would like to try. Again, there were no volunteers, and Vi began to wonder if anyone would ever use the elevator.

"Can I ride?" came a little voice from near where Vi and Mr. Archibald stood. Vi looked around and saw Polly Appleton stepping forward.

"I'd like to go into the sky," Polly said.

"Me too," said Mary Appleton, coming to her daughter's side. "We've watched the elevator building going up all these weeks. Now it's time we get to go up ourselves. Right, Polly?"

Violet's Bumpy Ride

"Right, Mamma," Polly agreed happily.

"Me too," said a raspy voice from another direction. Vi turned to see the elderly Widow Amos pushing people aside with her cane.

"It's fittin' for me and little Polly to try out this thing," Mrs. Amos croaked. "The youngest and the oldest—ain't neither of us got enough sense to be afraid. Besides, I got a hurtin' in my back, and I need to get to the clinic right quick."

Then Dr. Bowman spoke up: "The elevator will carry four, and I'd like another ride. So if you ladies don't mind, I'll join you."

The four passengers entered the tall structure and stepped onto the elevator platform. Mr. Archibald closed the steel gate, activated the hoist, and the elevator began its slow ascent. Everyone was silent as the strange-looking cage moved slowly upward. Then Polly began to giggle. And Mrs. Amos let out a shout: "Yippee, I'm flying! Like a bird leavin' the nest!"

As Vi watched, she heard several people begin to laugh. A man behind her said, "If the Widder Amos can fly, I might as well give it a go." Another man said, "Mr. Archibald built it, and he's the best. I wanna go up in that thing." A woman said, "It makes a lot of noise, but it seems safe enough. I'll ride it."

When the elevator reached the second floor, it stopped with a loud clunk. They were all looking upward when Mrs. Amos leaned over the railing and called down.

"That's the best fun I've had since my husband took me to the circus. And that was thirty years ago!"

Her words got everyone laughing, and within minutes, people were lining up to take rides. Mary and Polly came

down by themselves, and Mary pulled Vi aside, saying, "That was amazing, but I got work to do. It seems like we're having a little party here. I baked this morning, so I have a bunch of cookies made. I can fix lemonade, if that's all right with you."

"It's a grand idea," Vi responded. "People can have their rides and then come inside for refreshments. And thank you, Mary. If you and Polly hadn't —"

Mary put up her hand and said, "It was all Polly's doing. I'd never have gone on that thing on my own."

"Where is Polly?" Vi said. "I want to thank her."

Mary pointed to the line where Polly stood with Mrs. O'Flaherty.

Smiling proudly at her child, Mary said, "She's waiting for another ride, and it looks like she's talked Mrs. O into taking it with her."

Vi was astonished. Mrs. O'Flaherty had always supported Vi's determination to build an elevator, but she'd finally confessed that her one true fear was of heights. She knew it was not reasonable, but still, Mrs. O had been adamant about her own intention to continue using the stairs. Yet here she was, waiting her turn for a ride and looking quite pleased at the prospect.

A bit of verse from the book of Hebrews came to Vi: "signs, wonders, and various miracles..." She thought, *I know that it's not a miracle, Lord, yet for Mrs. O to take the risk and ride the elevator — it is a wonder to behold! Your "perfect love drives out fear", and that is always a miracle.*

Violet's Bumpy Ride

The morning after the inauguration of the elevator, Vi drove her buggy to Miss Moran's house, where the lady was waiting. They went on to a building in the city, to an office on the second floor. Ed Travilla was already there. He had not met Miss Moran before, but his gentlemanly good manners won her trust instantly. In a few minutes they were shown into an inner office, and Ed introduced Miss Moran to his family's lawyer, Mr. Coburn, a somber-looking, middle-aged man wearing a dark suit and bushy side-whiskers.

They all sat at a large table, and the lawyer presented a document to Miss Moran.

"Please read it carefully," Mr. Coburn said. "I will answer any questions you have. I want you to be satisfied that everything is correct before you sign."

"You as well, little sister," Ed said as the lawyer handed a copy of the same papers to Vi. "Read every word."

The men then fell silent as Vi and Miss Moran read. The document was not lengthy, but Miss Moran went over it twice before asking several astute questions. Satisfied by Mr. Coburn's answers, she requested a pen, and with great care, she wrote her name. Ed then signed, followed by a clerk whom Mr. Coburn had asked to witness the contract.

When the document was handed back to him, Mr. Coburn smiled and said, "You are pleased with this lease arrangement, Miss Moran?"

Returning his smile, Miss Moran said, "Very pleased. I retain ownership of my house, yet Miss Travilla will have full use of it for her mission. I don't know what you know about Wildwood, sir, but there's a terrible need there for shelter when folks find themselves without a place to live. So many fires, lots worse than my own."

130

Cleaning Up

She reached across the table and laid her hand over Vi's. She looked first at Vi, then at Ed, saying, "I know you will make good use of the house, my dears. Last night, I was thinking how pleased my mother and father would be to know that their house will be of service to others. They could have left Wildwood when the neighborhood went down, but they loved their home. Mamma said that if you have love for something, you don't abandon it when times are tough. That applies to people too. That's why I'm so happy. This lease lets me keep the house and know that it will be used to help people I care about. I can't thank you two young people enough."

"It is we who owe thanks," replied Ed, smiling handsomely. "And my good friend Professor Raymond. I predict that you are going to like working for him."

"Since he's your friend, I am sure I will," said Miss Moran with a little smile that made her look almost girlish.

Taking their leave of the lawyer, Ed escorted Vi and Miss Moran to a nearby hotel, where he treated them to an excellent luncheon. Vi told Miss Moran that Mr. Archibald had been engaged to construct a new kitchen and laundry to replace the buildings lost in the fire — news that added to the lady's delight. Then Ed chatted with her about Mark Raymond and his work. From her reading, Miss Moran had a vague notion of what archaeologists did, but the information Ed provided seemed to excite her imagination.

"I expected to feel sad about leaving my house," Miss Moran said at the end of the meal. "But, truth be told, I can't wait to meet the professor and his children and get to work." She nodded knowingly at Vi and added, "After all these years, I have a chance to live my early ambition to care for children. I hope I'm not too old to keep up with them."

131

Violet's Bumpy Ride

Vi laughed lightly and replied, "I hope that they can keep up with *you*."

Back at Samaritan House, having left Miss Moran at her home to complete her packing, Vi and Ed went to her office to go over a few business matters. While Vi was bent over her desk, adding up a long column of numbers, Ed went to the office window and stared out.

"Things are going well for you, aren't they, little sister?" Ed asked.

"Yes, they are," Vi replied, looking up at him. "We see more new people at the mission every day, and leasing Miss Moran's house will allow us to serve those in need of a place to lay their heads. I think that most of Wildwood now regards us as just another part of the neighborhood. That's what I've prayed for, Ed, that we should be regarded as friends here — not outsiders. And as you know better than anyone, we're managing to stay within our budget," she added with a laugh.

"You are," he said, "but I wasn't thinking so much about Samaritan House. I meant that *you* are doing well. Your — ah — your personal life. Mark and his children will be here in two days."

"They will," Vi said. She wasn't sure what her brother was trying to say, but she could tell that something was weighing on his mind. She sensed that what troubled him had little to do with her or Mark Raymond.

"How are you, Ed? How is your personal life?"

His first reply was a heavy sigh. Then he turned from the window and sank down in a chair in the corner.

"My life is fine," he said. "At least it should be. Ion is thriving, and I love my work. Farming suits me, Vi, just as it suited Papa. The family is well. You are well. I should be happy, but—"

He stopped speaking and looked to the window again, as if the trees outside might give him the words to say.

Finally, he returned his gaze to Vi and said, "It's Zoe. I can tell this to no one but you, Vi. I think—I'm almost sure—that I am losing my heart to her, yet I have no idea what to do about it. She is the most maddening girl. There are times when I think I have a chance with her. The other day she came to Ion with Grandpapa, and she and I went riding. It was a beautiful day, and we rode for miles. We went to that old cabin by the stream where the Ku Klux Klan had their headquarters. I told her about Papa and Grandpapa fighting against the Klan, and how Cal Conley really saved Ion by revealing the Klan leader's plans. Then she asked me lots of questions about the family and about my childhood. I've never felt so comfortable talking about myself with anyone. I even told her about when I accidentally shot Papa, and she really understood how that affected me. Then as we were riding home, I inquired about her recent activities, and she began talking about some house party she was invited to and how she would be going with Charlie Haynes and his sister. After that fight she and I had when you last visited Ion, I knew better than to say anything about Charlie. But just to hear his name on her lips infuriated me!"

Ed rose suddenly and went back to the window.

Turning away from Vi, he demanded, "Why should I care about Charlie Haynes? Why should I care about Joel Beckham and Sid Carter and Beau Mitchell and all those

other young dandies who are always fluttering around The Oaks these days?"

"I don't think you care about them," Vi ventured in a soft tone. Remembering something her mother had said, she continued, "I think you may be seeing rivals where there are none."

At this, Ed's head seemed to snap around, and his expression was full of confusion.

"Believe me, Ed, our Zoe thinks of Charlie Haynes and those other boys in exactly the same way I do — as friends," Vi said. "Should she not have friends?"

"Of course, she needs friends!" Ed declared in an impatient tone.

Vi knew her brother too well to be offended by his little outburst. He was angry with himself, not her.

"Are you in love with Zoe?" she asked.

So straightforward a question instantly deflated his ire, and Ed sat down again in the corner chair. He dropped his eyes and ran his hand through his hair. He didn't speak.

"I think that is the real question that troubles you," Vi said gently. "If you have lost your heart to Zoe, be glad, dear brother, for she is worthy of your love. The answer lies in your heart, Ed. If your feelings are true, then perhaps it is time to share them with Zoe."

"What if she doesn't feel the same?" he asked. "What if she rejects me?"

"Somehow I don't think that will happen," Vi said with a smile. "Besides, if you're too fearful of rejection to find out if your feelings are returned, then you can't really be in love, can you? Would you sacrifice the possibility of happiness to your pride?"

Ed looked up, and the anger was gone from his eyes.

"Do you think I have a chance with Zoe?" he asked.

"I can't speak for her, but I can tell you this," Vi said firmly. "If you do not tell her how you feel, you will have no chance at all."

"I don't know if I can find the words," he said.

"They're in your heart. Look there, and you'll know what to say."

Ed sat still and riveted his eyes on his sister. Then he surprised her by breaking into a grin.

"Will you tell me what words Mark spoke to win your heart?" he asked in his old teasing way.

Vi's eyebrows arched as she declared, "No, I will not! They are mine and his to treasure. Besides, brother, words are but the expressions of what we are and what we feel. If the feelings are true, the plainest words will be beautiful to the one who hears them."

Ed smacked his knees in a jovial gesture and then stood. He came to Vi and laid his hands on her shoulders. "Thanks, little sister," he said, "you've given me hope."

"The Lord blesses those 'who put their hope in his unfailing love,' " she reminded him, quoting Psalm 147. "Talk with Him and let Him be your strength. That is how you will know what is right for you—and for Zoe. I know that you have always turned to your Heavenly Friend in times of doubt. He is there to guide you now."

"I know, Vi," Ed said. "I think I should pray for His help in restraining this awful pride of mine."

"You might also ask forgiveness for thinking ill of Charlie Haynes and those other boys," Vi said with a smile. "They aren't at fault in this. How could they help being charmed by Zoe, though she does not seek their attentions?"

"Indeed," Ed said. "How could they help being charmed? They're all good fellows, and they don't deserve to be the object of my anger. I've been holding Charlie and the others accountable for my own failing."

There was an earnest tone to his voice as he added, "I *must* ask forgiveness, dear sister, now that I see how unfair I have been. You were teasing me, but you've put your finger squarely on my problem. *I* am the author of my frustrations, not Charlie Haynes—and certainly not Zoe."

"Then let God help you erase those feelings," Vi said, "as an author erases words that he has written in error. You won't be happy until you do."

He leaned down to kiss the top of her head, saying, "When did you become so wise? I thank the Lord for blessing me with such a remarkable sister. You've given me hope today—and a much-needed dose of reality.

"Now tell me one more thing before I go," he went on in a lighter tone. "Have you and Mark set a date yet? Should we be planning on a summer wedding?"

"No and no," Vi laughed. Then she sobered and added, "Though we haven't spoken of this before, you know how I feel about Mark. It seems that I am an open book. I can tell you that he feels for me as I do for him. But I don't want to encourage talk of a wedding, even in jest. Such a decision depends on others besides just Mark and me."

"You mean his children?" Ed asked. Then he answered his own question: "Of course, you do. They're going to love you, Vi. I'm sure of that."

The smile came back to Vi's face.

"I hope so," she said. "I hope they will."

8

The New Residents

*By faith he made his home in
the promised land like a
stranger in a foreign
country. . . .*

HEBREWS 11:9

The New Residents

*I*n Mark's most recent letter from Kingstown, he asked that Vi come to the railway station to meet the Raymonds on their arrival in India Bay. "Do you realize that it has been more than three months since I was in India Bay?" he had written. "Please humor me, and let yours be the first face I see when we alight there."

Vi wanted more than anything to meet Mark's train, yet a little inner voice warned her that this might not be the best idea. She worried that her presence could seem intrusive to the Raymond children. They would surely be exhausted by the trip and might resent having to meet new people the minute they stepped off the train.

But when Vi talked it over with Mrs. O'Flaherty, her nagging internal voice was soon hushed.

"Vi girl, it is possible to over-think such a situation," Mrs. O said in a tone of mock sternness. "What could be more natural than meeting them when they arrive? If you were in their place, wouldn't you be comforted knowing that your father has friends in the strange city that is to be your new home? Besides, you won't be alone. Kaki will be with you."

"And you will go, won't you, Mrs. O?" Vi asked.

"If you want me to," Mrs. O'Flaherty said with a warm smile. "We shall form a small welcoming party. You can drive the carriage, and Enoch will drive the cart. I am sure the Raymonds will have a large amount of luggage. The train is coming in mid-morning tomorrow, isn't it? And you know as well as I do that the station is dreadfully crowded at that time. Shouldn't good friends spare Mark the trouble of finding and organizing cabs to transport his children and all their belongings to College Street?"

Vi smiled at this. "I can always trust you to bring me down to earth," she told her friend. "It makes perfect sense when you put it in practical terms. I must remind myself more often of Grandmamma Rose's advice. Mark's children need loving and thoughtful friends. With God's help, I will become more than a friend. But that lies in the future, and the future is not mine to control."

Vi's inner voice of doubt was silenced by this conversation, though for reasons she could not have guessed, it had not been entirely wrong.

Mrs. O'Flaherty was right about the crowds at the India Bay station. The next morning, she, Vi, Kaki, and Enoch stood on the platform waiting for the train to pull in. All about them, people — some arriving from distant locations, some anxious to leave, and others like themselves waiting to greet friends and loved ones — were jostling and bumping into one another in what seemed like pure chaos.

The day was already hot, but under the lofty tin-roofed shed that covered the tracks and walkways, the temperature soared. The noise was worse: an ear-splitting cacophony of ringing bells, shrill whistles, churning engines, mechanical poundings, and raised voices. In the midst of this confusion, railway conductors in neat blue uniforms moved calmly up and down the platforms that ran between the tracks, calling out information about arrivals and departures and giving directions to harried travelers.

Since one could only be heard by shouting at full voice, Vi and her companions chose to wait quietly. When a round little man bumped Vi with his very large suitcase, he stopped and said something she could not hear, but his expression told her he was apologizing. She nodded, smiled sweetly, and watched as he seemed to be swallowed up in the crowd.

A minute later, a conductor passed close enough for the group to catch his words: "Number 37 from New York, Washington, Richmond, and points between! Arriving now at Platform Three!"

"That's it!" Kaki exclaimed.

She said something else, but it was drowned out by the repeated shrieks of a whistle and a roaring that shook the platform like an earthquake. Slowly, the great black locomotive pulled into the shed, its iron wheels grinding to a stop at the station end of the tracks. People stood back as a burst of steam rose like a thick, white cloud from the engine. Puffs of steam continued to rise from beneath the train cars, elevating the temperature and humidity inside the shed even higher.

There was no way to know which car the Raymonds occupied, so the welcoming party moved as close as possible to the train. They walked down the platform and searched each window for Mark Raymond. Their progress was slow, since the passengers getting off the train were moving like an ocean wave in the opposite direction.

Vi saw him first, in the middle compartment of the fourth car from the engine. Her heart began racing, and she wanted to run to meet him, but the crowd made running impossible. Still, she hurried her steps as much as she could and began waving.

Violet's Bumpy Ride

When Mark spotted her, a look of such sheer delight spread over his face that it brought tears to Vi's eyes. She wanted nothing more than to rush into his embrace, but she was quickly reminded that Mark was not alone. He disappeared for a moment, and then reappeared with a small child on his arm. Vi knew it had to be Gracie—as delicate and beautiful as a china doll. She bounced up and down on her father's arm, and white-blonde curls bobbed gaily under the rim of her bonnet. Her cheeks glowed, and her pretty mouth opened wide with gleeful excitement.

In that instant, Vi fell in love with a second member of the Raymond family.

Mark made a broad gesture with his free arm, pointing toward the open door at the rear of the carriage. In seconds, Vi and the others were standing at the doorway, and Mark and Gracie emerged.

"Miss Travilla and Miss Kennon!" Mark called out as he descended the narrow metal steps to the platform.

Seeing the maid, Gracie threw her arms wide and cried, "Kaki! Kaki!"

Kaki put out her own arms and took the little girl into her embrace.

Mark turned back to the door and reached for another, older child. Lulu's braids swung out as her father lifted her from the train to the ground. She was also smiling, but Vi caught something else in the child's face. A coolness? Or was it wariness? More likely, Vi thought, it was just fatigue after the long trip.

Mrs. O'Flaherty stepped forward and said, "I believe you are Miss Lulu Raymond. My name is Mrs. O'Flaherty, and my friends and I are very pleased to welcome you to India Bay."

Lulu remembered her manners well enough to make a polite curtsey in reply. But her curiosity was stronger than etiquette, and she said in wonderment, "You have a gold tooth, and you sound like Kaki."

Mrs. O'Flaherty threw back her head and laughed heartily. "I like you, Miss Lulu," she said with a wide grin. "I like it when people speak their mind. You are correct. Kaki and I sound alike because we both come from Ireland. And I do indeed have a gold tooth. Someday I'll tell you how that came to be."

Mark missed this little exchange. He was busy helping Max from the train and, with Enoch's assistance, taking the luggage that the porter handed down to them. When they had assembled the bags on the platform, Mark made a quick set of introductions. Lulu and Max grabbed their own light valises, and Kaki, still holding Gracie, took the child's small travel bag. Lulu held Mrs. O'Flaherty's hand, and even Max willingly accepted Vi's hand. Mark found a station porter, who put most of the remaining bags into a pushcart. Then Mark and Enoch hoisted the last of the suitcases, and everyone fell into line behind the porter.

The crowd on the platform had thinned somewhat, so the walk to the vehicles parked on the street outside the station was not too difficult. The bags were quickly loaded into the cart, and Enoch asked if Miss Lulu and Master Max might like to ride with him. With a nod from their father, the two youngsters were soon perched on the high seat of the cart with Enoch between them. Enoch told them they would be following behind Miss Violet's carriage.

Lulu was surprised when she saw Vi climb up to the carriage driver's seat and take the reins.

Violet's Bumpy Ride

"Does that Miss Violet know where our house is?" Lulu asked Enoch.

"She sure does, and so do I," Enoch said. "We'll be there in about twenty minutes. Could make it in half the time if we didn't have such a load."

"What's it look like — our house?" Max inquired.

"Why, I don't want to take the fun outta your surprise," Enoch answered. "But I can tell you this. Your Papa made a mighty good choice. Now, you two hang on tight to those little side-rails. This seat's on springs, and it bounces good. But if it bounces *too* good, one of you might get bounced all the way up into a tree, and I'd have to climb the tree and get you down, like rescuing a cat."

Lulu looked up at Enoch and squinted her eyes in an expression of disbelief. "That couldn't really happen, could it?" she asked.

"Anything's possible," Enoch said. His tone was serious, but the corners of his mouth were twitching, as he struggled to keep from laughing.

"I don't think we could bounce into a tree," Lulu said flatly. But she grabbed the side-rail anyway and didn't let go until they reached the house on College Street.

Mark hardly recognized the house he had leased; it looked so different from the dusty, empty place he had toured in the winter. Vi had written to him that Kaki was doing a splendid job of cleaning the place, but she had not given him many details. The bright rooms and the comfortable arrangements of his furniture nearly overwhelmed him with gratitude.

The children were just as astonished. They wanted to see everything at once, but first they met Miss Moran, who was waiting with sandwiches and cookies and cool drinks for the travelers. They ate as if they had not had a bite in days. Then Miss Moran and Kaki took the children and Mark on a guided tour.

Lulu decided that she was glad Enoch had not described the house. Every room was a surprise, and even their father's furnishings, which were now familiar to the children, looked like new in this setting. There were also things that Lulu didn't recognize, and when they went to see the bedrooms upstairs, she was too amazed to speak.

The stairway landing formed a wide hall in the center of the second floor. Kaki led them to the first of three doors along one of the side walls. They knew instantly whose room it was, because the walls had been painted and decorated in Gracie's favorite colors.

Gracie's room was a rosy pink, and curtains of a creamy white with a pattern of pink rosebuds fluttered at the open window. Her bed was made of polished brass, and her own little rosewood chair sat near the window. A child-sized desk and chair, a tall wardrobe, and a chest of drawers completed the furnishings.

The second room had to be Lulu's because it was the same shade of apple green as her very favorite dress—a birthday gift from her papa when she was nine. Lulu's curtains were creamy, like Gracie's, but had a pattern of butterflies in various poses and in some places nesting in what appeared to be the branch of a cherry-blossom tree. Lulu had never seen such a pretty room, and she was thrilled to realize that it contained *two* narrow iron beds, painted a crisp white and dressed with pale blue coverlets embroidered in white. *If I ever have a friend*, Lulu thought, *she can come and stay the night with me!*

The third room had been decorated for a boy who read stories of adventure. The walls were an ocean blue, and the curtains were white with a wide blue band along the edges. The bed was made of sturdy maple, and there was a bookshelf and a desk of the same wood. But what caught Max's eye before he really noticed the walls and the furniture was a large model of a four-masted sailing ship that rested on a stand atop the bookshelf. It looked just like some of the ships he'd seen in Boston Harbor. Max had often gone to the harbor when he could get away from his aunt's house, and he'd imagined himself setting out on a ship just like the model.

Located on the opposite side of the hallway, Mark's room was plain in comparison to his children's, but Kaki explained that she hadn't known the professor's taste and so she'd thought it best to leave the walls white until he decided on a color.

The fifth upstairs room was very small and had been left bare of furniture. "It could'a been a baby's room at some time," Kaki said to the professor, "but I didn't know how you wanted to use it. So we just cleaned it and put up them white curtains."

"We might need it for storage for the time being," Mark said. "You've done a superb job, Kaki. Just superb. I do not know how you accomplished so much in such a short time. And the children's rooms…"

He turned to Max, Lulu, and Gracie. "Do you like your rooms?"

"Yes, Papa. Yes, yes, yes!" they shouted.

"What made you think of painting them in our favorite colors?" Max asked Kaki.

"Why, that was Miss Vi's idea," Kaki replied. "She asked if I thought you'd like it, and I was sure you would. I thought I had the right colors, from knowing you up in Boston. Did I pick right?"

Again the children answered with happy yeses.

"But what about the things we've never seen before," Max said, "like the sailing ship in my room?"

"Ain't that a beautiful thing?" Kaki said. "Well, let me see now. The rugs and extra furniture come from Miss Vi's mother, Mrs. Travilla. She said you don't have to keep them, but they'll serve till you can get your own things. That ship model's a gift to you, Max, from Mr. Ed Travilla. It was made by a cousin of his who's in the U.S. Navy."

"Who's Ed?" asked Lulu, who had been only half listening.

"I've told you about the Travillas. Don't you remember, Lulu? Mr. Ed Travilla is one of my very best friends," her father replied. "It was to visit Mr. Travilla and his family that I first came to India Bay."

Max poked his sister's arm and said, " 'Member, Lulu?"

"Oh, yeah, the Travillas. I just forgot for a minute," Lulu said, not quite hiding the annoyance in her voice. Poking her brother once for good measure, she walked off.

"I want to see my room again," she said.

"Come downstairs in about ten minutes," her father told her. "Miss Violet and Mrs. O'Flaherty will be leaving, and we all want to thank them for everything they've done."

"I will," Lulu said airily as she entered her room.

I'll say good-bye and good riddance, Lulu thought as she walked around her bedroom, opening the wardrobe doors

and looking inside her desk and chest of drawers. She tried to find something not to like about the room, because it had been Miss Vi's idea, but it was still the prettiest room she could imagine.

She plopped down on the bed closest to the window, pulled off her shoes, and sat cross-legged on the soft coverlet. *It may have been that lady's idea, but Kaki did all the work, so she's the one I should thank. Not that Miss Violet.*

Lulu lay back on the pillows and gazed upward. The sunlight coming through the trees outside made patterns on the ceiling. As Lulu watched the shifting light, her conscience got the better of her, and she told herself that Miss Vi had been nice to get all this work done for them.

Maybe she is just a good person. I really like Mrs. O'Flaherty, and she's Miss Violet's friend. So I guess I might like Miss Violet sometime. And it's only fair to give her a chance. She didn't try to be bossy or act like anybody's mother today, so maybe she's okay. Besides, I can't be mean to her 'cause that would hurt Papa.

The bed was so comfortable that Lulu turned on her side and snuggled against the pillows. She closed her eyes and listened for a minute. A bird was chirping somewhere near her window. She wondered if it were a bluebird. She thought about a woman with a gold tooth and a buggy that could fly to the tops of trees and a boat that could sail on a sea of cherry blossoms and…

Someone was shaking her gently.

"Wake up, sleepyhead. You've snoozed through lunch and part of the afternoon."

Lulu rolled over and rubbed her eyes with her fist. A figure sat beside her on the bed.

"Papa?"

"Yes, dear. I hate to wake you, but I was afraid to let you sleep any longer. You might not be able to sleep tonight, and then your clock would be turned upside down."

Sitting up but still a little confused, Lulu asked the time, and her father told her that it was almost three o'clock.

"Gracie is having her nap," Mark said, "but Max is anxious for you to go outside with him. He has been exploring the garden and found a few things he wants you to see."

"Like what?" Lulu asked. She was fully awake now and feeling quite hungry. "Can I have another sandwich first? Miss Moran makes good sandwiches."

"Kaki saved your lunch," Mark said, "and Max is waiting for you. Miss Moran put your clothing away while you were snoring, so you might change into a play dress."

"I don't snore," Lulu replied with a grin. Looking down at her rumpled travel outfit, she said, "I will change my clothes. This dress is all hot and sticky."

"Can you do the buttons by yourself?"

Lulu gave him a funny look and said, "Of course I can, Papa. I'm not a baby."

Mark went to her door. "Come down when you're ready," he said. Then he asked, "Are you very sure that you don't snore?"

His daughter was laughing when he left the room.

After her lunch, which she ate in the kitchen while she talked with Kaki and Miss Moran, Lulu dashed outside. Her brother was sitting on the front steps.

Violet's Bumpy Ride

"Papa said you found something you want me to see," Lulu said.

Max jumped up and said, "You're gonna love this place. Come on."

He bounded down the steps, and Lulu followed him.

"The grass is nice," she said, skipping on the springy lawn.

"The back's better," Max said. He led his sister around the far side of the house to what was like a grove of trees. "There's three old maples here. They're the trees we see out our windows. And look at this!" Max exclaimed, running to the largest tree.

Hanging from a high branch was a wooden seat suspended by two thick ropes.

"A swing!" Lulu cried.

"It's new, too," said Max. "Mr. Enoch made it, and he cut some of the tree branches so we could swing higher. I'll give you a push."

Lulu got onto the seat and grabbed the ropes. When she was settled, Max took hold of the ropes and pulled her as far backwards as he could. Then he let go, and Lulu went speeding forward. She screamed with pleasure as the swing lifted her toward the leafy green branches of the old tree.

"Pump your legs," Max called out, "and you'll go way up!"

Lulu knew what to do, extending her legs and then drawing them in—a steady motion that increased the height and the speed of the swing. As the swing curved back toward the ground, Max stepped away, and Lulu swung backwards. Lulu kept her back and forward movement going for several minutes; then she stopped pumping and let the swing slow down on its own. At last she stopped it by dragging her feet on the ground.

"What about that?" Max asked.

"It's not at all like the swings in the park," Lulu said as she caught her breath. "I never went so high before! I wanted to let go and just fly."

"Don't you ever do that!" Max said sternly. "That's one of Papa's rules. Always hold on with both hands. Don't stand up in the swing. And be sure that no one is near you when you start swinging. You can start somebody off, like I did, but then you have to move away real fast. And never jump off before the swing stops moving."

Lulu, who never liked rules, listened to her brother but wasn't paying close attention.

"What's next?" she asked.

"There's a garden in back," Max said, leading the way again. "There's nothing much in it right now, but Papa's gonna hire a gardener, and he said you and me and Gracie could have a place to plant. He said we could grow our own vegetables."

At the rear of the property, the children saw a large structure with two huge doors but no windows.

"That's the carriage house and stable," Max said. "Papa's gonna buy a carriage or a big buggy. He's not sure which, but he says he has to make his mind up fast, 'cause we need transportation."

"That means he'll buy a horse too!" Lulu exclaimed. "And we can learn to ride it!"

A whole world of possibilities had just been opened for her. She followed Max to a small grazing pasture behind the stable, but her mind was already seeing herself atop a sleek Arabian pony that ran like the wind. Together they would dash off to hunt for treasures on the plains or in the desert.

Violet's Bumpy Ride

"Over here," Max was saying. He pointed to a hedge of tall boxwood bushes at the far side of the pasture. "This is the best of all."

Lulu couldn't think why her brother cared about some thick old bushes. They hardly compared to her rich fantasies. But as she watched, Max approached one of the boxwoods, dropped to his knees, and scurried underneath. Lulu ran to the spot where Max had stood and got to her knees.

There was an opening, and she could see Max sitting inside the bush. Crawling through the opening, she felt like a mountain explorer entering a cavern. But instead of a rock cave, this one was formed of thick branches that curved out and formed a green canopy over her head. The thick leaves made the space dark and cool, but there was enough light for Lulu to see. The space was about four and a half feet tall at the center of the bush. The ground was littered with pieces of wood that crunched when Lulu stepped on them.

"It looks like the lower limbs got damaged somehow," Max said. "Or maybe somebody cut them off. Anyway, that's what made this big hole."

"It's like a big, round, green tent," Lulu said. "How did you find it, Max?"

"I was walking around and I saw a fat rabbit in the little pasture," he said. "I tried to sneak up on the rabbit, to get a closer look, but it musta heard me. It hopped away real fast, right into these bushes. I followed it, and I was looking for its rabbit hole when I saw the opening under this bush."

"Oh, we can't tell anyone about this," Lulu said in an excited whisper. "It can be our very own secret place, can't it? We can clean out all these old sticks and leaves and make it real nice."

152

Max liked this idea, though he wasn't sure why it should be a secret. But he knew how Lulu enjoyed make-believe, and he thought it would be fun to share a secret with her.

"We should tell Gracie," he said.

"Oh, we will," Lulu agreed. "But let's get it cleaned up first. We can come here every day when she's having her nap and fix it up. It'll be such a good surprise for her."

Max didn't know how much cleaning a patch of dirt under an old bush needed. Still, he was willing to go along with Lulu, and it would be fun to surprise Gracie.

"Do you like being here in India Bay?" he asked Lulu. "Do you like the house?"

"The house is really beautiful," Lulu said. "I don't know about India Bay yet, but I already like having a place where we can play."

"Our rooms are great," Max said. "Kaki and Miss Vi and Mrs. O'Flaherty worked so hard for us."

In the shade of their "secret place," Max couldn't see the scowl that suddenly came over Lulu's face. She forgot all about her earlier intention to give her father's friend a fair chance, and Max heard the unpleasant tone in his sister's voice as she replied, "I know our Kaki worked hard. And Mrs. O'Flaherty and Mr. Enoch. But I don't expect a grand lady like that Miss Violet did much to help. I don't expect she ever does real work."

"Why do you say *that* Miss Violet' in such a mean way?" Max demanded. "You never saw her before today, but you're always so snippy when you say her name."

Max didn't normally challenge his sister, but Lulu was being cruel and sarcastic and that bothered him.

"I'm not snippy!" Lulu exclaimed defensively.

Violet's Bumpy Ride

"You are, too," Max said in a low, hard tone. "Miss Vi is a very kind lady, and she's Papa's friend. She went to a lot of trouble to make the house so nice for us. You've got no reason to be hateful about her, and you'd better stop it before Papa catches on. I don't like it when you act like this, Lulu. I'm going back to the house."

Max scrambled out of the opening in the bush, but Lulu sat where she was. She knew that her brother was angry with her, and she didn't like it.

"Okay, Max! I'll be better," she called to him, hoping she sounded apologetic. Then she crawled out, expecting to find Max waiting for her. He never stayed upset with her for very long. But when she emerged from the hiding place, Max had gone. She looked up and saw him running toward the stable. He rounded the corner of the barn-like structure without looking back.

She stamped her foot on the ground. Scrunching her mouth into a tight knot, she made her ugly face, which Max called her "mad look."

"It's all *her* fault," Lulu said out loud because there was no one around now to hear her. "I don't care how pretty and nice she is. And I don't care how much you like her, Max Raymond. That Miss Violet will *never* be my friend!"

Angry tears fell from her eyes as she set off to the house.

"Max, you just don't understand," she argued as if he were walking beside her. "You just don't understand why I can't ever like her and be her friend. We have a mother. She's in Heaven but she's still our Mamma, and she loves us the same as ever. We don't need another mother."

Lulu swiped at her tears with her fist.

"I won't let Miss Violet or any other lady take our Mamma's place. I just can't!"

CHAPTER

9

The Sweetest Reunion

*Love and faithfulness
meet together....*

Psalm 85:10

The Sweetest Reunion

The next morning, Mark left his house immediately after breakfast with his children. He found a cab at the corner of the wide boulevard that intersected with College Street, and gave directions to the driver. His destination was the home of Dr. Kincaid, the elderly classics professor whom Mark would soon be replacing at India Bay University. Mark and Dr. Kincaid would consult frequently in the coming days, as the senior gentleman's official retirement day approached.

From Dr. Kincaid's, Mark took another cab to the center of the city, where he had an appointment with the bank manager, followed by a meeting at the office of Mr. Coburn, the lawyer. After seeing Mr. Coburn, Mark stopped in at City Hall. His business at each of these places related to his status as a new citizen of India Bay and the transfer of his affairs from Kingstown. It was all very important, but to Mark, each appointment kept him from his true destination.

He had told Vi that he would come to Samaritan House at about two o'clock, however another cab dropped him off in Wildwood some five minutes after the hour. Vi was standing on the porch. In violation of all rules of ladylike etiquette, she ran down the steps and across the drive to him. Oblivious to the curious stares of people at the mission, she fell into his arms. Mark clasped her in a warm hug, and they both laughed with joy at being together. But they suddenly became conscious of a woman and two children who were walking through the mission's open gates.

Grinning, the woman said, "Don't mind us, Miss Vi. We just come to see Doc Bowman. You go on with whatever you're doing."

The children were giggling as their mother pushed them toward the mission doorway. Vi looked at Mark and saw that he was grinning as well.

"Oh, dear," she said, looking flustered as he released her.

"Does this mean our secret is out?" he asked.

Vi's famous dimpled smile was all the answer he required. She looped her arm through his and led him toward the house. But instead of going in the doorway, she directed Mark to a path that wound around to the north side of the mission.

"You want me to see the new elevator?" he asked curiously. He had not expected his welcome to include a guided tour.

"Yes, I do," she replied gaily, lowering her voice and leaning close to him. "It will give us an opportunity for some private discussion," she said with a smile as they noted all of the faces watching them.

After the tour, the professor spent the next hour seeing his old friends at the mission and hearing their news. Vi had something to attend to in her office, so Mark went upstairs to find Dr. Bowman. Mark was surprised to learn that the young physician was now devoting five full days a week to the clinic. The doctor had given up most of his duties at the hospital, and he was planning to set up his own practice in Wildwood at the end of the summer.

There were more changes since Mark's last visit. Though Vi had written him about all the new developments, Mark was happy to see them in action. Mary and Christine were in the kitchen, preparing the mission's afternoon meal. While they cooked, they told him about the success of the home visiting service. When Alma Hansen came to help serve the meal, she happily informed the professor that her dear brother would be coming to live in India Bay in July.

"Your English is so much improved, Miss Hansen," Mark said.

"It is thanks to Mrs. O'Flaherty," the girl replied. "A very good teacher and friend she is to me."

Mrs. O'Flaherty, whom Mark found in the combined meeting-dining room, greeted him and asked about his children. Since they'd had little opportunity to talk the previous day, he inquired about her latest doings. She showed him her new piano, which stood at the far side of the large room.

"I am giving music lessons again," Mrs. O told him, "and we have started a children's choir. At this point, the children are more loud than musical, but they will improve. We have decided to give our first performance on the Fourth of July—a program of patriotic songs. Then you can judge for yourself how well we are doing."

"But I must miss your choir's debut," Mark said with obvious regret. "I leave for Mexico in the last week of June, and I shall probably be in the jungle of the Yucatan on Independence Day."

"We'll invite your children to attend in your stead," Mrs. O'Flaherty smiled. "Yesterday, your Max expressed his interest in visiting Samaritan House. I hope you will bring all three here very soon."

"I shall," the professor replied.

Mrs. O'Flaherty was just inquiring about Miss Moran when Vi entered the room. She held some sheets of paper in her hand and was smiling brilliantly.

"Good news?" Mark asked.

"Wonderful news!" Vi exclaimed. "This letter is from my cousin Virginia. She and the ladies of her club want to join us in our work here, and they propose starting a kindergarten for the youngest children."

"They will raise funds for such a project?" Mrs. O'Flaherty questioned.

"Yes, and much more. They want to operate the kindergarten and do the work themselves," Vi said. "Virginia says that they would like to meet with us next week."

"What a blessing," Mrs. O'Flaherty said softly. "What a blessing for the mothers and fathers of Wildwood. Perhaps Virginia and her friends will inspire others who have much to be generous to those who have little."

"What do you mean?" Mark inquired. "I thought the mission had a number of wealthy benefactors."

"We do," Vi said. "We receive financial donations, but this is our first offer of real labor from anyone in the upper levels of India Bay society."

Vi consulted the letter and said, "Virginia writes, 'My friends are not naïve about this undertaking. They know that they have no experience with the kind of work required, and they are anxious for your guidance. Vi, I really believe that this project is not a whim and that you will find my friends to be attentive students and reliable volunteers. We have discussed our own weaknesses, and we are, to a woman, ready and willing to learn how we can help the parents and children of Wildwood.' "

"Do you know Virginia's friends?" Mark asked.

"Most of them," Vi said. "They are all older than I, so it seems strange to think of myself as their teacher. Mrs. O, I think you should fill that role, if you have the time, and I can be your assistant."

"I'll make the time," said Mrs. O'Flaherty without a second's thought.

People were beginning to arrive for the afternoon meal, and many glances were cast at the tall, sandy-haired man who was talking with Violet and Mrs. O'Flaherty. A few of the people had seen Mark on his previous visit to the mission, and they speculated that he might be a visiting preacher or doctor.

Seeing that Mark was the object of so much conversation, Mrs. O'Flaherty decided that he and Vi could use some privacy. So she said that she, Mary, and Alma would serve the meal, and she suggested that Vi take their guest upstairs to the schoolroom.

Vi started to protest, but Mark caught a wink from Mrs. O.

"I should like to see the progress you've made in the schoolroom," he said in a tone that was both professional and a bit louder than necessary. "I understand that Mr. Fredericks has acquired some new maps since I was last here."

Vi now realized what Mrs. O'Flaherty was up to and gladly played her part in the little charade.

"Yes, Professor, he has added some maps and a new set of geography books," she said. "I'm sure you will find them interesting."

Vi and Mark departed, and the people at the dining tables thought they had the answer to the question of who the tall man was. It seemed clear enough that he was a teacher—maybe a friend of Mr. Fredericks. It was also logical that Miss Vi would want to show him the schoolroom. So speculation ceased, and everyone turned their attention to the kitchen door and the entry of Mary Appleton, who was carrying a steaming kettle of her chicken and dumplings.

It was true that the schoolroom now included some handsome maps and new textbooks, and Vi quickly pointed them out to Mark.

"Now, sir, you have seen what you came to see," she teased.

"I have," he replied, "yet I cannot see enough of her. Oh, Vi, I have waited so long for this day. The letters you wrote were wonderful, but no substitute for the real you."

As Vi watched, his expression grew serious, and his blue eyes darkened.

He took her hand and spoke in a tone of such urgency that it took Vi's breath away.

"I have something to say to you that I haven't said before," he began. "But I have thought it every hour of every day that we have been apart. You know that I love you, Vi. I love you from the depth and breadth of my heart. I cannot imagine my life without you." With earnestness in his eyes, he asked, "Will you agree to be my wife? Will you marry me?"

Vi was not surprised by his proposal; over the months apart from each other, their letters had progressed to words of love. But hearing him actually say the words at last, her heart was flooded with a joy so great she could not contain it. "Yes, yes, yes! I will marry you, my darling professor. More than anything in all the world, I want to be your wife and love you for the rest of my life."

He drew her closer. Vi had never felt so beloved in all her life. All the love she felt from Mark, she returned with her whole heart.

The Sweetest Reunion

For each of them, time seemed to stop. The schoolroom, with its clutter of desks and its smell of chalk dust and furniture polish, vanished. It was as if they existed outside of the real world, in their own space and time, unaware of everything except their love for each other. Their whispered words were as soft as rose petals. They both shed happy tears, yet neither noticed.

When Vi looked up, Mark was smiling in that slightly off-center way that she adored.

"I had planned a more romantic proposal," he said. "I had practiced a speech of such eloquence that it would sweep you off your feet."

"You did sweep me off my feet," Vi replied with a laugh.

"Dearest darling, are you sure that you wish to take me on? I'm not the easiest person, as you know. I am not one of those fancy-free young suitors among whom you could take your pick. I'm not —"

She cut him off by putting her fingers to his lips.

"You are everything to me," she said.

"And I am not so easy myself," she went on in a laughing way. "Why, I am known for being headstrong."

"But always in a good cause," he said. "I love your boldness and courage. Remember, my dear, that I have seen you in action. I fell in love with you on that day you confronted Mr. Greer in the Wildwood Hotel. I never knew that a woman could be so angry and so beautiful at the same time. And do you remember the first letter you wrote to me in Kingstown? I was mired in self-pity and guilt, but you had the courage to scold me. You'll never know what a kindness that was, for you made me understand that many of my worries were selfish."

"I didn't say that you were selfish," Vi protested.

"No, but I remember that you used the term 'self-indulgent.' What you wrote made me think long and hard and reconsider my course. I changed because of you, and my children and I have begun to build our relationship because you, dearest, set me straight."

"When will you tell the children about us?" Vi asked. Suddenly, this seemed the most important question they were facing.

Mark echoed her concern when he replied, "Not for a while. I think that you and they deserve the opportunity to get to know one another. I have no real concern about Gracie. She longs for a mother, for she barely remembers her own. Max and Lulu will need more time, I think. But as they see more of you, they will soon grow to love you as I do."

Vi said gravely, "I never want them to think that I'm trying to replace their mother. Though I'd marry you this very minute, we must put Max and Lulu and Gracie before our own desires. I hope and pray that they will love me, but I want them to trust me. It would be a betrayal of their trust to expect them to accept me into your family without fair warning."

Mark had to laugh. "You make yourself sound like one of those prairie tornadoes that drops out of the clear blue sky. Oh, my dear, kind Vi. Do not doubt yourself or my young brood. You will earn their trust soon enough, and their love will follow. We just need to proceed slowly at first, especially with Lulu. She is the least trusting of the three."

"Do you know why?" Vi asked.

"I can't be certain, but I believe it is my fault. She was not quite six when her mother died and I, for all intents and purposes, abandoned her. No—don't make excuses for me. Without realizing what I was doing, I caused her to suffer two terrible losses when she was at a very impressionable age. In a way, she became stronger. Lulu is far more inclined to take risks than Max, and she will dare almost anything to protect him and Gracie. She has a quick temper, but I have come to see that she is also the most sensitive and easily hurt of my children. Trusting is hard for her, because she is so afraid of being hurt again."

"Does she know the Lord? Does she find comfort in His love?" Vi asked.

Mark didn't answer for some moments. Then he said, "Lulu goes to Sunday school and church every week; she reads the Bible and learns her verses without complaint. She prays with us. I cannot fault her religious observance, yet I can't say that she has invited Him into her heart. The truth is that each of my children is still somewhat of a mystery to me. Unlike her brother and little sister, Lulu holds her own feelings close. She is a frank and honest girl—too frank at times—but she is slow to reveal herself to others."

"She is young," Vi said softly, for she knew instinctively that she had touched on a subject that troubled Mark. "She has been through a lot for a child of her age."

Mark stepped back from Vi and took hold of her hands. He looked into her eyes as he had before—deeply, searchingly. Then he smiled again.

"How good God is to me," he said. "How glorious is His plan for us! I truly believe that He led me to you, my darling. Lulu is not the only Raymond who knows the fear of being hurt. After the shock of my wife's death, I thought that I could detach myself from emotion, and even from my faith. Until I met you, Vi, I denied my feelings because that seemed the surest way to avoid the pain of loss and grief and guilt. In my fear and arrogance, I disobeyed our Lord's command to love others. But I could not deny the power of my feelings for you. Even if you hadn't returned my affection, you would have brought me back to a truth that I tried to ignore — I am capable of love, and I need to love others. Loving you was the jolt I needed. I have been restored to our Heavenly Father, and in His wisdom, He has returned me to my children."

Mark pulled Vi into his arms and said, "The weeks and months ahead may be difficult for us. We have a family to build, and I know that I cannot do it alone. I need your strength, my darling, but I want to be fair to you."

"Then do not doubt my dedication to making our new family," Vi said, laying her head against his shoulder. "We will build our family upon the rock of our Lord and Savior, and with His help, we'll strengthen one another. My parents taught me that marriage is a partnership, and that partners must share in everything — the difficult times as well as the good. That's what I want — to share everything with you on the journey ahead."

"Our path is sure to have its ups and downs," he said with a low chuckle. "Experience tells me that even the best of marriages is a bumpy ride."

"I can handle whatever comes, as long as you are at my side," Vi said.

Mark cradled the back of her head in one hand and her chin in the other. Gently, he lifted her face upward to his and gazed into her sparkling eyes.

"Our journey together begins today, darling Vi," he said softly.

CHAPTER

10

Another Day at the Mission

There is a time for everything,
and a season for every
activity under
heaven.

ECCLESIASTES 3:1

Another Day at the Mission

*B*efore leaving the mission school-room, Vi and Mark had agreed on two things of immediate importance. First, they would tell only Mrs. O'Flaherty and Vi's mother about their plans to marry. They were not trying to be secretive, but they felt that no others should hear the news before Max, Lulu, and Gracie did.

Secondly, they decided that the children should be invited to visit the mission before Vi went again to the Raymonds' home. This was Vi's idea. When she met Mark's children, she had sensed Lulu's reserve. What Mark had told her about his middle child affirmed her feeling. She thought that a day at the mission, a working day, would give her the chance to be with the children in a setting far less intimidating than a formal gathering for tea or supper. Max could meet Seth Fredericks, who would be one of his teachers at the Boys' Academy. Gracie could play with Polly. And Lulu might enjoy helping Vi and Mrs. O'Flaherty and the other residents. At least that was the plan.

When Mark told his children about Miss Vi's invitation—set for the Tuesday after their move to India Bay—Lulu seemed no less enthusiastic than Max and Gracie. Lulu had little idea what a mission was, and being a very curious girl, she wanted to visit Samaritan House and learn what happened there. She also hoped to see Mrs. O'Flaherty and Enoch again, for she liked them both. And ever since Max had chided her about her attitude toward Miss Vi, Lulu's conscience had been troubling her. She'd told Max that she would act better, and Lulu honored her promises. She had decided to try her hardest to be nice to Miss Vi.

Meanwhile, Max and Lulu spent their first days in India Bay exploring their house and neighborhood. There were, as their father had promised, a number of children living in the comfortable family homes along College Street. Max soon met a couple of boys his own age. One of the boys had a sister who was a year younger than Lulu, and the children played together on several occasions.

Gracie, after so many years of being denied the company of other children by her aunt, was shy about making friends, so she spent most of her time with Miss Moran. Being much wiser than most people suspected, Miss Moran quickly realized that Gracie was not naturally timid; rather, the little girl needed time to adjust to her new surroundings and equally new freedom. "Gracie'll make friends more easily," Miss Moran told Kaki, "if we let her do it at her own speed."

By the day of their visit to Samaritan House, the three young Raymonds were ready for an outing. The first Tuesday of June was a fine, sunny day. Right after breakfast, Mark and Max went to the stable to hitch the family's newly purchased horse to their new buggy. Miss Moran checked the girls' neat but simple attire—pretty cotton play dresses and crisp white pinafores—and gave their hair a final primping.

At about the same time that the residents of Samaritan House were beginning their daily tasks, Miss Moran and Kaki stood on the front porch of the white house on College Street, waving good-bye as Mark and his children departed for their trip across the city.

"I hope those youngsters won't be disappointed by Wildwood," Miss Moran said. "They've probably never visited such a poor neighborhood."

"I don't think it'll bother them," Kaki replied. "When they were livin' with their aunt, it was in the finest part of Boston. But except for Miss Gracie's fancy clothes and some toys, those children didn't get many luxuries from Miss Marsh."

"I'd like to know more about their lives before they came here," Miss Moran said thoughtfully as the two women went back into the house.

"I can tell you what I know," Kaki said. "And the professor's open about most things. It might help you to hear what they've been through. They haven't had it easy—the little ones or their papa. Does me heart good to see 'em all so happy here. I'd sure hate for anything to upset 'em now that they're finally coming together as a family."

Over the past week, the people who came regularly to the mission had gotten used to seeing the tall professor. After his daily meetings with Dr. Kincaid, Mark would come to Wildwood Street for an hour or two, and without any special effort, he was making a good impression. He was always friendly, and he willingly helped out where he was needed— carrying supplies down to the cellar for Miss Vi, stacking firewood with Enoch, sitting with little Jacob when Christine was busy. Word went around that Professor Raymond was a new teacher at India Bay University, and someone got the idea that he was making a study of the mission. When that rumor spread, most people agreed that it was good to have an important professor taking an interest in Wildwood. Other than Miss Vi and her family, prominent people were rarely seen in the neighborhood.

Violet's Bumpy Ride

When the four Raymonds arrived at the mission, everyone immediately surmised that they were a family. All three children had their father's light hair, blue eyes, and lean frame. The boy looked just like his daddy, but it was the middle child—the girl with the braids—who had the professor's distinctive smile, just the tiniest bit off center.

Vi and Mrs. O'Flaherty greeted the visitors and showed them inside. The children were surprised by the size of the house; they had expected it to be smaller, cramped, and maybe dingy. They were silent for a time, taking in the spaciousness of the entry hall with its elegant curving stairway and then the big, sunny room filled with long tables and dozens of chairs.

"This is our main room," Mrs. O'Flaherty said. "It used to be two parlors, but now it is where we meet and eat together."

"There's an awful lot of chairs," Max said. "How many people live here?"

"Right now, there are eight people who live at Samaritan house," Vi explained. "The chairs are for the people who come here every day to share our meals and our devotions. Upstairs, we have a schoolroom, a little nursery for the youngest children, and a clinic where our good doctor and nurse work. On the third floor are five bedrooms."

"Who sleeps up there?" Lulu asked.

"I do," said Vi. "And Mrs. O'Flaherty and Miss Hansen, who is a wonderful seamstress. She made the curtains and bedspreads for your rooms. When we have overnight visitors, they use our guestrooms. Your friend Kaki stayed with us before she moved to your house."

Mark was standing back, pleased that his children were showing such interest in the mission.

Gracie spoke next, in a small voice that betrayed her shyness. "Do any children live here?"

Vi knelt down and took the child's hand. "I'm glad you asked," Vi said. "Our family includes a little girl of your age, and she is anxious to meet you. Her name is Polly Appleton, and she lives downstairs with her mother, who cooks all the food we serve."

"She's six years old, just like me?" Gracie asked.

"She celebrated her sixth birthday here at the mission, and her mother made the most delicious cake for her," Vi replied.

Gracie's eyes opened wide as she said, "I was six in April, and Papa got a 'licious cake for me too."

"Then you and Polly already have something in common," Vi said, smiling.

Without considering her movements, Lulu had come to stand beside Vi.

"Does Mr. Enoch live here?" Lulu asked. "Did you know about the swing he made for us? If he's here, can we tell him 'thank you'?"

"He'd like that very much," Vi said, turning her dimpled smile to Lulu. "Mr. Enoch and his family live in a house behind the mission. His wife, Christine, is our housekeeper, and their son, Jacob, is the youngest member of our household. He's two years old."

Max was about to inquire how many people came to the mission, but he held his question when the kitchen door opened and a lady in an apron entered.

"Good! Our guests are here!" Mary Appleton called out cheerfully. "Maybe you young'uns can help me. I made gingerbread cookies for the schoolchildren's lunch today, but I ain't sure how good they are. Would you three give 'em a taste for me?"

Violet's Bumpy Ride

Max, Lulu, and Gracie looked up to their father with questioning eyes.

"I'd accept Mrs. Appleton's offer, if I were you," Mark said with a grin. "I have enjoyed her cooking several times, and I'm sure her cookies will be a treat."

Gesturing to the children, Mary said, "My girl Polly's in the kitchen waiting to see you. Come on now, while the cookies are warm and the milk I poured is cold."

The children needed no further encouragement. They ran to Mary.

When the kitchen door closed behind them, Mark reached down to Vi and helped her to her feet.

"Well, we seem to be off to a good start," Mrs. O said.

"Indeed," Mark said, smiling at Vi. "Are you sure you don't mind if I leave for a while?"

"Not at all," Vi said. "We'll be fine. You can tell the children good-bye and go on to your meeting with Dr. Kincaid. You will return for lunch with us?"

"I will try, though my good mentor sometimes keeps me longer than I anticipate," Mark replied. "Don't delay eating if I am late."

"We shan't, though I hope he will not keep you too long," Vi said.

"Do you think you might need me here?" he asked with concern.

"Of course, Vi needs you," Mrs. O'Flaherty chuckled. "But not to mind Max, Lulu, and Gracie. Go with a light heart and return as soon as you can. Your children are in safe hands."

Another Day at the Mission

When the children had finished their milk and cookies, Vi and Mrs. O took their young guests on a tour, introducing them to the other residents of the mission and to the people who were waiting to see Dr. Bowman. Polly joined the group, and by the time they had seen the whole house, she and Gracie were giggling together and chatting away as if they had always been friends.

Seeing how well the little girls were getting along, Mrs. O'Flaherty suggested that they go to the nursery with her. She thought that Polly could show Gracie the books and toys kept there and that they might enjoy doing some drawings.

Vi asked the older children if they would like to see the new elevator, and of course, they did. But Vi needed to attend to some matters in her office first. If Max and Lulu would come with her, she would introduce them to another resident. This made Lulu very curious, for Miss Vi had said that eight people lived in the mission. Lulu counted the eight people they had already met—Miss Vi, Mrs. O'Flaherty, Mrs. Appleton and Polly, Mr. Enoch and his wife and son, and Miss Hansen. Had Miss Vi made a mistake?

"I don't understand. You said eight people live here, and we've met eight people," Lulu said. "We also met Dr. Bowman and Miss Clayton, but I didn't count them because they don't live in the house."

"Your arithmetic is correct, Lulu. Eight people live at the mission, but we have nine residents. It's a riddle, isn't it?" Vi replied with a mysterious smile.

They had come to the office door. Vi led them into the small room and pointed to the window.

"Our ninth resident is in her favorite spot on that window ledge," Vi said. "Her name is Jam. If you gently stroke

her back and speak softly at first, I know she will be your friend."

Max and Lulu had never had a pet; their Aunt Gert had declared that all animals were unhygienic and should not be tolerated in any house. At first the children only stared at the orange-striped cat, for they were not sure how to approach her. Then Lulu stepped to the window, walking on tiptoe. Cautiously, she put out her hand and ran one finger lightly along Jam's back. When the little cat purred, Lulu looked anxiously over her shoulder at Vi.

"She's purring because she likes your touch," Vi assured the girl. "Keep stroking her like that, Lulu. Once she is used to you, I'm sure she'll want to play."

Lulu continued running her fingers over the cat's furry back. Max joined her and spoke to the cat. "Hello, Jam," he said. "You're a very pretty cat. You're so orange. I've never seen such an orange cat. You look like a furry pumpkin."

Jam clearly enjoyed Lulu's tender strokes and Max's compliments. After a couple of minutes, the cat stood, stretched, and hopped from her perch to the floor.

"She wants to play," Vi said. From a drawer in her desk, she took a ball of yellow knitting yarn and handed it to Lulu.

"Roll this across the floor and see what she does," Vi said.

Lulu and Max both sat down on the floor, and Lulu pushed the ball toward Jam. The cat batted it back with a swift move of her paw. Lulu laughed out loud and again rolled the ball to the cat.

While the children played with Jam, Vi turned her attention to several pieces of mail lying on her desk. She was glad to see a small white envelope among her business correspondence. It was from her mother. Vi laid this envelope

aside and opened the other letters. There were several bills and a letter from Mr. Coburn regarding the lease of Miss Moran's house. As she scanned the letters, Vi was conscious of the children playing near her feet, and with relief, she sensed their growing ease with her.

Since none of the business letters required an immediate answer, Vi opened her mother's letter and began to read.

"Oh, no!" she exclaimed.

Max's and Lulu's heads popped up. They saw that Vi's expression had changed entirely. There was less color in her complexion, and tears glistened on her eyelashes; her hand was trembling slightly as she read.

"What is it, Miss Vi?" Lulu asked anxiously. "Are you all right?"

Still gazing at the letter, Vi said, "Yes, I'm all right. But I have received some sad news. This letter is from my Mamma, and she tells me that a very dear member of our family has died."

"Who?" asked Lulu, remembering that Vi had brothers and sisters.

"My great-great-aunt," Vi said in a sorrowful tone. "Her name is Miss Wealthy Stanhope, and she lives—lived—in Ohio."

"We're so sorry, Miss Vi," Max said. He tried to think of something else to say, but no comforting words came to his mind.

Vi took a handkerchief from her pocket and wiped her tears away. Then she looked down at the children and smiled—a beautiful smile that conveyed something more than sadness.

Vi's smile stunned Lulu. The only death Lulu had ever experienced was the devastating loss of her mother, and she

recalled how all the adults had cried and carried on at the funeral—Aunt Gert worst of all. She assumed that was how adults were supposed to act. Lulu hadn't cried then, but she hadn't smiled at anyone. For a very long time, she felt sick and hollow inside, like a part of herself had been cut out and taken away. Even now, being reminded of that awful, awful time, the sensations came back—knotting her stomach in a brief spasm of pain.

How can Miss Vi smile when someone is dead? She hardly has a tear to spare for her aunt, Lulu thought angrily. *How can she brush her tears away and be so coldhearted?*

"Aren't you sad?" Lulu blurted out. "Aren't you sorry your aunt's gone and is never coming back?"

Vi didn't seem to hear the harshness in Lulu's voice, but Max did.

Vi sighed heavily. She bent forward, and her shoulders slumped, as if some heavy load had been placed on her back.

"I am sad, very sad, because I loved my Aunt Wealthy, and I will miss her so much," Vi said. "She was an extraordinary woman."

"Maybe you could tell us about her," Max said, hoping to make up for his sister's strange behavior. "When my mother died, it sometimes made me feel better to talk about her."

Vi considered for a few moments. Then she said, "Yes, I would like to tell you about her. I think you'd both have liked her."

Vi proceeded to speak of Wealthy Stanhope's long and fascinating life—how she had been born in 1780, shortly after the United States had been born; how she had traveled to exotic places as a young woman; how Wealthy had once lived on the frontier with some of her family. She told them about Wealthy's home in Ohio and how she had raised an orphaned niece and, some years later, a nephew. Vi recounted her own first visit with Wealthy, when all the Stanhope relatives had descended on the small town of Lansdale to celebrate their Aunt Wealthy's one-hundredth birthday.

Listening to Vi, Lulu's anger disappeared almost as quickly as it had appeared. She even found herself laughing when Vi described Wealthy's odd habits of speech and her unusual style of dress.

"I guess you'll miss her a lot," Lulu said, as much to herself as to Vi.

"I will," Vi agreed, "but I know that she is happy. Aunt Wealthy is with the Lord at last, and that is her eternal reward for a life of faith in Him. She wasn't afraid of dying, because she knew that death is just the beginning. With all her heart, she put her faith in Jesus and His promise—that 'whosoever lives and believes in me will never die.'"

Vi looked down at the letter that she was holding. "I will grieve for our loss," she said, "but not for my Aunt Wealthy. She is with our Heavenly Father. Her unwavering faith in His promise is now fulfilled."

"But how do you know that she's really happy?" Lulu asked.

Vi could see in Lulu's eyes that this question was not an idle one. Vi leaned forward and stretched out her hand. Instinctively, Lulu took her hand and felt the young woman's warm fingers close over her own.

"I know because I believe," Vi said. "The Bible says that 'no eye has seen, no ear has heard, no mind has conceived what God has prepared for those who love him.' I believe

this applies to us on this earth and when we die and go to be with Him in Heaven. Our imaginations cannot even conceive of the possibilities. My Aunt Wealthy loved the Lord very much, and she was eager about going to Heaven. I'm sure God has exceeded her expectations, much to my beloved aunt's delight."

With her hand still in Vi's, Lulu tried to imagine what Heaven might be like. Still holding Vi's hand, Lulu stood. Despite so many weeks of believing Miss Vi to be an enemy, at that moment, she felt no trace of fear or mistrust.

"Thank you both for being with me," Vi said in a low, sweet tone. "Talking about my aunt has reminded me to rejoice in her life and all the gifts of love and friendship she bestowed on others."

Vi pulled Lulu a little closer as she went on: "When my Papa died, I was just a few years older than you and Max. I never doubted that Papa had gone to be with God, but I had such terrible feelings of fear and loss and guilt. For many months, I couldn't even cry for my Papa, and I wouldn't tell anyone except God how I felt. Yet even in my prayers, I tried to hide my true heart. It was so hard, but I learned a lesson I never want to forget. God truly is our greatest Friend, and He is always there to hear our sorrows and ease our pain. He also gives us the comfort of our earthly family and friends, if we are willing to share with them. I didn't know how much I would need friends today, yet God knew. Later today, I will tell Mrs. O'Flaherty about Aunt Wealthy. I will try to be as good a friend to her as you have both been to me."

"Will Mrs. O'Flaherty be very upset?" Max asked. Though he'd seen Mrs. O'Flaherty only twice, he had grown very fond of the plainspoken, good-humored Irish lady with the gold tooth.

"I don't think she'll be upset," Vi replied with confidence. "When a person is blessed, as Aunt Wealthy was, with a hundred and four years of life, her passing is not a shock. Mrs. O will surely feel as I do—sad about the loss of someone we loved dearly but joyful that she is now with our Father in Heaven."

"I'm sorry that you have to feel sad, Miss Vi," Lulu said, compassion welling up in her heart. "But I think I understand how you can be happy too."

Vi smiled, and her dimple appeared. "Human feelings can be so confusing," she said. "How can we be sad and happy at the same time? How can we dislike someone we don't really know? How can we be angry with someone we love? Your father tells me that you both read your Bible. I'm so glad, because God has given us His Holy Word to answer our questions and end our confusion. Tonight, Mrs. O and I will spend a lot of time with our Bibles, taking solace in His Word—and that's just what my wonderful Aunt Wealthy would have us do."

By now, Max was also standing, and Jam—finding herself neglected—had gone back to her accustomed resting place on the window ledge.

Vi glanced down at her watch.

"Oh, my," she said. "It's almost high noon, and Enoch will be waiting to give you a ride on the elevator. The Bible tells us that there is a time for everything. Aunt Wealthy never wasted time feeling sorry for herself. I can almost hear her, saying for me to pull up my socks and get on with living. She might have said 'sock up your pulls' in her tumbled way, but I always understood what she meant."

Lulu didn't realize that she was still holding Vi's hand when they left the office and went outside to find Enoch.

Violet's Bumpy Ride

But as the day went on, Lulu observed Vi more closely than she usually attended to adults, other than her father. She saw the sadness that came into Vi's soft, dark eyes when others weren't looking. Little by little, Lulu's heart seemed to be opening to the young lady who, like herself, knew the hurt and fear of losing a parent.

Vi was also observing. Mark's youngsters were full of questions, and Vi noticed how often their queries focused on the problems of the people served by the mission. Their interest in the welfare of others was warming to her heart.

At one point, after Alma had shown them the clothing that she was repairing for people in need, Lulu asked Vi, "Why are there so many poor people? It's not fair, is it, Miss Vi?"

"There are so many reasons," Vi said with a small sigh. "We learn every day of parents who have lost their employment and cannot support their children. We feed people who work but earn so little that they can't afford good food. At the clinic, we help people who are too ill or too badly injured to work. Do you remember the Widow Amos? She spoke to you outside the clinic."

Lulu nodded and said, "She's a nice old lady. She said she liked my freckles."

"Well, Mrs. Amos worked all her life, and by herself she raised her family after her husband died. Now she's elderly and can't work. Her only support is her grandson, who works at the livery stable. Our mission is to serve people like Mrs. Amos. I can't say that life has been fair for her, but I believe that all lives are equally valuable to God. In His eyes, the people here in Wildwood are the same as the richest people in the land."

Lulu pondered what Vi had told her for some moments. Then she said, "It just doesn't seem right. If God loves everybody the same, why do some people have such hard lives?"

"I wish I could give you a simple answer, but I can't," Vi responded. "I do know this — God loves everyone without distinction. He commands us to do the same, to love our neighbors as ourselves. When Jesus said that, He wasn't telling us to love just the people who are *like* ourselves. I don't know why some people suffer more than others, but I know that we are commanded to help one another. When we put our faith in God and truly believe what Jesus taught us," Vi said, "then we will live by His example. That's what we're trying to do at Samaritan House."

"You do good works here, Miss Violet," Max said. "I can see that."

"But I still don't know why some people have to be so poor," Lulu said a little fretfully. Lulu wasn't trying to be difficult. Her heart had been touched by many of the people she'd met at the mission, and her strong sense of fairness was challenged. She looked at Vi with wide, questioning eyes.

"I don't know either," Vi said thoughtfully. "It's part of faith to accept that God has a purpose for each of us, including those who are poor. I can understand how you feel, Lulu. I've struggled with this question myself."

Lulu began to think that maybe Miss Vi really could understand her feelings. She took Max's and Lulu's questions seriously and was willing to talk with them about important things. And Miss Vi was ready to admit when she didn't have an answer. *She's sort of like Papa that way*, Lulu thought with a little jolt of surprise. *He explains things, and he tells us when he doesn't know something. That's how Miss Vi is treating us. She doesn't think our questions are silly.*

That afternoon, Lulu left the mission with a lot to think about. She had promised Max that she would *try* her hardest to be nice to Miss Vi. But a funny thing had happened; Lulu didn't have to try. It was easy to be nice to Miss Vi, because Miss Vi was so nice.

After breakfast the next morning, Lulu went straight to the "secret place" in the bushes behind the stable. Max had gone off to find one of his new pals, and Gracie was accompanying Miss Moran to the market. So Lulu had the morning to herself.

Lulu and Max had cleared the little cave of broken branches. They had removed all the sticks and dead leaves and then made a floor of straw from the stable. After a couple of days, they had shared their secret with their father and Gracie and shown them the hidden spot under the boxwoods. Mark had thanked them for including him in the secret. He made them laugh when he promised not to tell any of the other professors at the University.

"Those gentlemen are forever looking for a quiet place to read and study," Mark had said. "If I told them about your comfortable hidey-hole, you might come here to play and find your special place occupied by some gray-bearded old scholar and his books."

"Papa, what's that word—'hidey-hole'?" asked Gracie.

"It's just an expression for a place like this—a hide-away," Mark said.

Lulu earned laughs when she responded, "Well, we cleaned it up and made the straw floor. So it's a *tidy* hidey-hole!"

Now, on the day after the visit to Samaritan House, Lulu was sitting cross-legged on the floor of the hidey-hole. She rested her elbows on her legs and propped her chin on her fists. This was the position she preferred when she had important thinking to do.

Miss Vi isn't at all what I imagined, ran Lulu's thoughts. *She's very pretty, but like a real person is pretty. Her hair keeps falling out of its pins, and she wears eyeglasses when she reads. That's not perfect. And she wears ordinary clothes and aprons. I like that. I guess she could dress up like a princess if she wanted to. She could wear fancy dresses and diamond tiaras and stuff, but that would make the people who come to the mission feel bad. Miss Vi cares an awful lot about how other people feel. She's not selfish like me.*

Lulu shifted her position and brushed back some stray strands of hair that had come loose from her braids. *I wish I hadn't spoken so rudely when she told us about her great-great-aunt. Miss Vi was really, really sad. I could tell by her eyes. It was nice of her to tell us about her aunt. I wonder what she'd think if I told her about Aunt Gert.*

Lulu began to consider the other members of the Travilla family. She'd met Miss Vi's big brother when Edward visited the Raymonds a couple of days after their arrival in India Bay. *He was just as nice to us as Miss Vi. I could see how much Papa likes Mr. Edward. Papa should have a good friend.*

Then Lulu remembered Mr. Edward saying that the Raymonds should come and visit his farm soon. She hoped that would happen. Lulu had never seen a real farm before. Besides, now that she had met Miss Vi and Mr. Edward, Lulu was more curious than ever about their family.

Violet's Bumpy Ride

She was imagining the Travillas' farm. All her ideas came from the stories she read, so she pictured a farmhouse and a barn, with chickens and maybe pigs running around a dusty yard. She thought they might have apple trees and cows. Then she began to imagine herself as a farm girl, and she thought that perhaps a girl could have some real adventures on a farm.

Lulu pushed her wrong ideas out of her mind and decided not to think about them. After the visit to the mission, Lulu could no longer see "Miss Vi" as the terrible, scheming woman she'd created in her imagination. But Lulu couldn't entirely dismiss her fears and mistrust. She wasn't ready to admit her own mistake and seek forgiveness. So she tucked her bad feelings away, in a place deep in her heart where they were out of sight and out of mind.

CHAPTER

11

A Startling Conversation

*For the ear tests words as
the tongue tastes food.*

JOB 34:3

A Startling Conversation

The visit to the mission had gone so well that Mark wondered if his concerns might be groundless. The children, including Lulu, spoke glowingly of their experiences, and they all seemed quite taken with "Miss Vi," as well as the other members of Samaritan House. Max talked excitedly about the elevator and the discussion he had with Mr. Fredericks about the Boys' Academy. Lulu seemed amazed by the many services provided at the mission. More than once, she said, "I don't know how Miss Vi and Mrs. O do it. Aunt Gert never worked that hard at anything." And Gracie chatted endlessly about Polly Appleton—her very first friend in India Bay!

Mark was so encouraged that he decided to accept an invitation that had come from Ion. Elsie Travilla had written to ask the professor and his children to spend the following Sunday with her family. She noted that Vi and Mrs. O'Flaherty would also be in attendance.

Mark might have sent his regrets, if the day at the mission had not gone so successfully. But now he felt confident that his youngsters would enjoy themselves. So early on Sunday morning, the Raymonds set out on the buggy ride to the country. It had rained the night before, but the morning sun quickly dispelled the dampness, leaving everything smelling fresh and clean. As they left the city, they began to see fields planted with row upon row of sturdy seedlings and large pastures carpeted in tall grass. For a little while, the children were quiet as they drank in their first sight of the Southern countryside. But after a quarter hour or so, they started to bombard their father with questions. It wasn't long before Mark's knowledge failed him.

"I'm very sorry, but I just don't know exactly how tall corn grows or how a cow is milked or how butter is made," he laughed. "Your father is a teacher, not a farmer. Fortunately, Mr. Edward is a very good farmer, and I'm sure he can answer all your questions."

"But you always know everything, Papa," Gracie said.

"No human can ever know everything, my dear," Mark replied, "not even your Papa. Only our Lord has perfect knowledge. A wise person — man, woman, or child — should never feel shame in admitting his ignorance, as long as he is willing to learn. So I admit to you that I am almost entirely ignorant of modern farming."

He looked down at Gracie, who sat beside him, and added, "I am as curious as you about corn growing and cow milking and butter making."

From the back seat, Lulu asked, "Isn't it dumb to be ignorant?"

"Not at all," Mark said. "To use your word, it is 'dumb' to pretend that we know something that we do not know. However, I hope you will not use the word 'dumb' anymore. It's not a kind thing to say of anyone."

Mark's rebuke was very mild, but he wanted his children to understand the power of words to inflict pain and hurt. He was also trying to cure both Lulu and Max of the habit of using slang, which they had acquired in Boston.

"Is it a rude word?" Lulu asked.

"Not always," Mark said. "See those goats in the field over there? We might call them 'dumb animals' because they do not have the power of speech. We may use the word to mean 'silent.' But to say that a person is 'dumb' or 'stupid' or any disrespectful word because they do not know something is very unkind. Do you understand?"

"Yes, Papa," Lulu replied. "I'd get mad if somebody called me 'dumb.' It would make me feel bad."

"Then let's agree not to use the word to describe anyone."

Lulu thought it might be hard never to call anyone 'dumb' again, because she thought that some people, like her Aunt Gert, were dumb. But Lulu wanted to please her father, so she would try her best.

The horse and buggy was nearing Ion, moving along at a leisurely clip, when suddenly a large rust-colored horse appeared beside them. Gracie shrieked in fear, but she started giggling when she recognized the rider on the horse's back.

"Mr. Edward!" she called out.

Mark reined his horse to a stop. "Where did you come from?" he asked his friend.

"From behind you," Ed grinned. "I saw this buggy heading toward my home, and I thought it might contain our special guests. So Galahad and I raced to catch up with you. I apologize for giving you a fright, Miss Gracie."

"Is Galahad your horse?" Gracie asked.

"Yes, he is, and if you agree, Galahad and I will be your honor guard—your escort to Ion. Mother and the others are coming in the carriages and shouldn't be too long. Our minister preached an especially lengthy sermon this morning, and I was afraid we would arrive at home too late to greet you. So I rushed ahead, and old Galahad didn't fail me."

Ed wheeled his prancing steed and took a position at the front of the buggy. He held the horse to a gentle trot, and the little procession moved forward.

"What a beautiful horse!" Max said.

"Edward is a superb horseman," Mark said. "All the Travillas are excellent riders, for their father set them on horseback almost as soon as they could walk."

"Even Miss Vi?" Gracie asked.

"Especially Miss Vi," Mark said with a soft smile that Lulu, seated behind him, couldn't see.

Lulu's imagined farmhouse and barn were as far from the reality of Ion as the North Pole is from the South Pole. The large, graceful home that came into full view as the buggy rounded a bend in the driveway was—in Lulu's eyes—a mansion.

Mark guided the buggy in front of a tall, white-columned portico, and two men came forward. One man helped the children to the ground and then took the buggy reins from Mark. Ed dismounted and handed his reins to the other man.

"I've given Galahad a good run, so he needs a longer cooldown than usual," Ed told the stableman. "When my mother gets here, will you keep her carriage at the ready? I'll be taking our young guests for a ride after lunch."

Turning to the Raymonds, Ed declared in a hearty voice, "Welcome to Ion!"

All three children had been gazing up at the estate house in wonderment.

"I thought this was a farm, with a barn and chickens and pigs and things," Lulu said in an awed tone. "But it's— it's a palace!"

"It is a great house, isn't it?" Ed said with justifiable pride. "But really, Miss Lulu, Ion is a farm. We have a barn—several of them—and stables for the horses. We have chickens, pigs, and other farm animals, too. If you three agree, I will take you for a tour this afternoon, and you can see that Ion is a hardworking farm, though probably larger than you expected."

"Oh, yes, please! I want to see everything," Lulu replied excitedly.

"Me, too," Max said with as much fervor as his sister.

"Can I go?" Gracie asked her father. "I've never seen a real piggy before."

Mark lifted Gracie up and said, "Of course, you may go. I'm sure you will see more than just one pig."

"Then we are all agreed," Ed said cheerfully.

He was telling them more about the farm when they all heard the clopping of hooves on gravel and the creak of wheels. Two open carriages and a buggy rounded the little bend in the driveway.

"They have finally caught up with us," Ed said.

The stablemen had reappeared, and Ed accompanied them to assist the passengers and attend to the vehicles.

The first person to step from the carriage was a tall, beautiful older woman dressed in an elegantly simple blue silk dress. She came to where Mark and the children stood.

"Hello," she said, speaking directly to the children. "I am Mrs. Travilla, and I am so happy that you could visit us today. Let me guess," Elsie said. She extended her gloved hand first to Gracie. "You are Grace, I think, though you like to be called Gracie. May I call you Gracie? It's such a charming name."

Gracie returned the handshake and managed a little curtsey as well. "Yes, ma'am, I'm Gracie," the delighted child said.

Violet's Bumpy Ride

Then Elsie introduced herself to Lulu and Max, who displayed excellent manners in return.

The other members of the family had gathered around their mother, and Elsie made a series of introductions. Lulu worried that she couldn't remember all their names, so she concentrated very hard. There was Rosemary, a pretty, round-faced girl who resembled Mrs. Travilla very closely, and Danny, a handsome boy not much older than Max. Then came two tall young men who looked exactly alike. They were the twins, Harold and Herbert, and Lulu could not have told them apart if they had not been dressed differently.

From the second carriage came Mr. and Mrs. Dinsmore, who were Mrs. Travilla's parents. They were accompanied by a blonde-haired young lady who seemed to Lulu as beautiful and delicate as a princess. This was Miss Love. When introduced to the young Raymonds, the young lady bid them call her "Miss Zoe" if they liked.

Finally, Vi and Mrs. O'Flaherty alighted from the mission's buggy and joined the group. Lulu was glad to see their now-familiar faces, for in truth, she was feeling overwhelmed by meeting so many people at once.

Elsie invited everyone to come inside, where their Sunday dinner was waiting. Mark carried Gracie and began talking to Mr. and Mrs. Dinsmore. The twins and Danny fell in with Max and put him at ease by conversing about the Boys' Academy. "Miss Zoe" was telling Rosemary something, and Mrs. O'Flaherty hurried to catch up with Rose Dinsmore.

Lulu followed behind, but she was by herself for only a moment. A soft hand touched her shoulder, and she looked up to see Miss Vi at her side. Lulu broke into a smile, which was as warm as it was spontaneous.

 194

A Startling Conversation

Vi bent toward Lulu and said in a confidential tone, "There are just too many of us for anyone to sort out my whole family at first. Perhaps you will sit beside me at the table, and I can give you a hint if you forget some of the names."

"Thank you, Miss Vi," Lulu replied with genuine relief and gratitude. "I don't think my head's big enough to hold everybody's names all at once. I'd like to sit with you."

"Do you know that I still forget?" Vi chuckled. "Harold and Herbert confuse me all the time, because they are so alike. When they were younger, they made a game of it. They'd each dress in the other's clothes. Harold looked like Herbert, and Herbert looked like Harold, and even Mamma would mix them up."

"That's funny," Lulu laughed. She imagined that it might be fun to be somebody else for a while — somebody who didn't cause mischief and who was just naturally good, like Gracie, so she didn't always have to try so very hard to be better. It was only a passing thought, and Lulu pushed it away. Today, she was happy being Lulu Raymond and the special guest of this big, friendly family in their amazing home. Lulu didn't want any dark thoughts to spoil the good feelings.

After their dinner, Ed took the Raymond children for the ride he'd promised. Zoe, Rosemary, Danny, and Mrs. O'Flaherty also joined the party, so Ion's largest carriage was packed with happy people when Vi and her grandparents waved them off.

"Where is the professor?" Horace Dinsmore asked his granddaughter. "I hoped to talk with him about a scholarly article I recently read."

Violet's Bumpy Ride

Horace didn't notice the blush that came to Vi's cheeks as she replied, "I believe Professor Raymond had something to discuss with Mamma. I saw them go to the library, but I doubt they will be long."

"I hope not," Horace said. "I really enjoy that young man."

"And his children?" Vi asked.

Her grandfather smiled and said, "They seem very well-mannered and quite bright. The little one — Gracie — is exceedingly pretty. I understand she has been ill, though she looks healthy enough."

"I think she was more frail than ill," Vi said. "But she has gained strength since going to live with her father. He is sure that she will continue to thrive in our warm climate."

"Ah, yes," Horace said, "I often wonder how anyone can stand the winters of the Northeast."

His wife laughed and said, "Yet I did well enough growing up in the cold winters of Philadelphia. Perhaps, my dear husband, you and I are merely showing our age. The sun of the South seems kinder to our old bones than the icy winds of the North."

"Bosh!" Horace snorted. "Old bones, indeed! Let us walk down to the lake, and I will show you how old my bones are."

Vi was glad to accompany her grandparents on their walk. She welcomed the diversion, which she hoped would take her mind off the conversation underway between the man she loved and her dear mother.

In the library, Elsie was seated on the couch near the fireplace, and Mark had taken the chair opposite her. With some amusement, Elsie saw how nervous he was. The normally confident professor could barely sit still. He clasped

and unclasped his hands, rested them on his knees, and then clasped them again.

"May I make this conversation easier for you?" Elsie asked in a gentle tone. "I believe that you wish to discuss your future—yours and Vi's."

Mark sat back more comfortably, though his expression was serious.

"I do," he said. Then quickly, he began to speak the words he had rehearsed: "Mrs. Travilla, I love your daughter, and she loves me. I hope you will give us your permission to secure our love in marriage. I know that you may have concerns. There are—ah—special circumstances— problems. My children—"

Elsie held up her hand and smiled as she said, "I have anticipated your request for some time, and I have also considered the circumstances. I do not believe that the problems will be too difficult for you and Violet. My daughter is an exceptionally mature and capable young woman."

Mark smiled too at the mention of Vi. "She is exceptional," he said softly, "though she seems entirely unconscious of her extraordinary qualities. She is so strong and yet so gentle. So beautiful and yet so lacking in pretensions. So rational in her thinking and yet so sensitive to the emotions of others."

"Violet is more like her father than my other children," Elsie said with the slightest trace of wistfulness. "I wish you had known him. He understood Vi better even than I. He used to say that of all our children, she would have to fly the farthest and soar the highest for her happiness. You need to understand that, Mark. Vi will not be passive. She needs to fly, and she needs a partner who will not attempt to clip her wings."

Violet's Bumpy Ride

"I would be a fool to try," Mark replied gravely, "for her spirit is God's great gift to her—and to me. You cannot know what she has done for me. I believe that she has given me back my life."

"Only God can do that," Elsie said.

"Oh, yes, I know," Mark replied quickly. "But your loving daughter showed me how long a distance I had traveled away from my Heavenly Father and His love. Through her, I was reminded where my true strength lies—in Him."

"Vi spoke to you of this 'distance'?" Elsie asked.

"She did," Mark said, "but long before she spoke, I was learning from her. I saw how she truly lives her faith every moment of every day. I'm a teacher. I know how important it is to inspire pupils to strive to do their best. But before I met Vi, I had lost the will and the confidence to be my best, except in my work. By her passion for helping others and her courage, she showed me the way back to myself and to the Lord. It was her spirit, Mrs. Travilla, that inspired me to re-examine my life and renew my own faith. I would never want to do anything to damage or restrain Vi's God-given spirit," he ended forcefully.

"I believe that. I believe you will support and protect one another," Elsie said, "and your children. You have answered the one question that I had in my heart. I have known for some time how deeply my daughter loves you. I knew, I think, even before she admitted it to herself. Now I see the same depth of feeling in you. So, yes, you have my permission to marry my daughter. You have more than my permission, Mark. I give you my blessing, in love and trust."

"Thank you, Mrs. Travilla," Mark said, his mouth breaking into a relaxed grin. "Thank you especially for your trust."

198

A Startling Conversation

Elsie rose from the couch, and Mark stood.

"I do believe that you and Vi have truly met your match. Your strengths complement each other," Elsie said with a beautiful smile. "With the Lord as your rock and your salvation, I expect that your life together will be quite an adventure. Now, shall we find our Violet and tell her of my verdict?"

Mark hesitated for a moment. Then he said, "Vi and I have agreed to tell no one but you and Mrs. O'Flaherty of our plans for the time being. We want to give my children time to get to know Vi first. Do you object to keeping our secret until we can tell the children?"

"I think you have made a wise decision," Elsie responded. "I will hold your secret until you and Vi tell me the time is right."

"It may not be a very long wait," he said. "I leave for Mexico in another two weeks. I wish I could change my plans, but my colleague is depending on me. While I'm away, however, Vi will use the time to get to know the children on her own. All three are very fond of her now, but both Vi and I think it may be easier for them to cement their relationship with me absent. By the time I return, I know that the children will love Vi as I do."

Mark was so confident, but at his last words, Elsie experienced the briefest instant of doubt. It flashed across the edge of her consciousness just as a mouse scurries so rapidly into its hole that human eyes can scarcely register its movement before it is gone. She would recall the feeling at another time, but for now, it was forgotten.

"Perhaps I should begin thinking of an engagement party in August," she said gaily.

Violet's Bumpy Ride

Ed's guided tour of the farm lasted two hours, and assuming the young Raymonds would be tired by the drive, he headed home. But Ed had misjudged the children. The ride and the stops along the way had invigorated them, and even Gracie declared that she had no need for her usual nap.

When the carriage approached the house, the children saw several people sitting on the veranda—their father, Mrs. Travilla, Miss Vi, Mark, and two young Negro girls. Mark rose and came to help the happy passengers from the carriage.

"I have a delightful surprise for you," he told his children. "Do you remember my telling you about the two children from South Carolina?"

"The girls that you and Miss Vi rescued from the bad man who wanted to steal their land?" Max said.

"Miss Vi did the rescuing," Mark said. "I just helped a little. They live at Ion now, and they want to meet you. Their names are Tansy and Marigold Evans. Tansy is the eldest."

The children followed their father onto the veranda, and Mark made the introductions. There were a few moments of natural shyness among the youngsters, until Rosemary stepped forward with the suggestion that they all come with her to the old upstairs nursery.

"Nursery!" Gracie exclaimed, looking quickly at Elsie. "Do you have a baby, Mrs. Travilla?"

"No, dear," Elsie replied. "My babies are all grown. The old nursery is now a playroom, with toys and games and books. Do you have a favorite plaything?"

"My paper dolls," Gracie answered quickly.

"Oh!" said Marigold. "We have lots of paper dolls! Would you like to see them?"

"Yes, please," said a clearly interested Gracie.

A Startling Conversation

Rosemary took Lulu's hand and then Tansy's. "Have you ever played *pachisi*, Lulu?" she asked. "It's a board game, and I love playing it. Would you like to try it?"

Lulu was nodding her head as Rosemary led the girls into the house.

Danny looked at Max and rolled his eyes. "There's more than just girls' stuff and games in the playroom," he said. "I have a telescope that you'd like. And binoculars. We could go up to the attic and look out. It's like being in a ship's crow's nest—almost. And no girls allowed."

The boys then marched off together, each of them very glad for the other's company when they were outnumbered by so many females.

The adults settled in for some quiet conversation. Then Elsie invited Vi and the professor to join her for a walk down to the lake. Vi had no objections to a second trek to her favorite spot; she already knew the results of Mark's meeting with her mother in the library, but she was anxious to hear the details.

Horace and Rose Dinsmore decided to visit with Aunt Chloe, and Mrs. O'Flaherty wanted to join them. Harold and Herbert had already left to ride to Roselands and see their great-grandfather and their Conley cousins. Soon, only Ed and Zoe were left on the veranda.

"That was a grand tour," Zoe said. "The professor's children enjoyed themselves immensely. You were very good with them—so patient with all their questions."

"They're really good kids," Ed said. "I told them to come back soon, and I'll get them on the ponies. They've never ridden horses before."

"It's because they always lived in the city," Zoe said, "as I did. But I learned to ride, and I love it."

201

Violet's Bumpy Ride

"You know, it's hard for me to imagine growing up in a city," Ed said, looking out over the fields of Ion.

"You're a country boy," Zoe said with a little giggle. "The life of a farmer suits you."

"Are you making fun of me?" Ed said.

"Not at all," Zoe said, fearful that she had offended him. "I think I have become a country girl myself since I moved here. When I first went to live with Uncle Horace and Aunt Rose at The Oaks, I couldn't sleep at night for the noise. It was so strange to me. Yet now I sleep like a baby."

"What noise?" Ed asked. "The city is noisy. The countryside is quiet."

"Not so quiet to ears that are accustomed to the sounds of carts and carriages on cobbled roads and people shouting in the streets. And cathedral bells pealing out the hours. And the roar of trains, and music and laughter all the night long. That's what I was used to in Paris and Rome. When I tried to sleep at The Oaks, it was so quiet that I could hear the house creaking and every rustle of the trees outside. It would seem so odd to you, but I'd never heard an owl hoot in the night. The first time I heard an owl, I jumped out of my bed as if someone had exploded a cannon in my room. I sat up in a chair the whole night, shivering like a baby. The next day, I told Uncle Horace about the horrible sound that had frightened me. When he explained that it was just an old hoot owl, I almost cried from my embarrassment. You would have had a good laugh at me."

"No I wouldn't," Ed protested, turning to look at her. "When you explain it, I understand. I have had the same trouble with city noises."

Zoe saw that he was not making fun of her as she often thought he was. She and Ed had such opposite reactions to

202

so many things, and it seemed to Zoe that she was forever explaining herself to him. They were oil and water, and Zoe had begun to wonder if it could be any other way. Would they ever be able to understand each other?

To halt this train of thoughts, she said in a light tone, "I heard some interesting news at the Featherstones' house party last weekend."

"I don't know why you still go to those house parties," Ed responded with a note of contempt. "They're just two whole days of gossip and more gossip."

"They are not!" Zoe exclaimed with a laugh. "Why, your Aunt Rosie and her husband were there as chaperones, and they were having a lovely time. Do you think they are just gossips?"

Ed sat down on an iron bench, resting his leg over one of the arms and turning his profile to Zoe. "So what interesting news did you hear?" he asked, making his tone as nonchalant as he could.

"It's about Diana Willoughby and Mark McCord," Zoe replied.

"I know that Di's been stuck on him since we were children," Ed said in a bored tone. "And he never batted an eye at her. When he got married and moved away, we all thought she'd forget him. But I don't believe she got over him. It's a shame about Mark's wife."

"Her death must have been very hard for him," Zoe said, "and their children."

Ed straightened himself and looked at Zoe. There was no more indolence in his tone as he said, "Mark is a sterling fellow, and he loves his children more than anything. It's been very difficult for him. He's moved back here for their sakes, to give them a real home."

Violet's Bumpy Ride

"Well, now they may be getting a new mother," Zoe said, revealing the news that had circulated at the house party.

"Don't tell me Di's got her hooks into him!" Ed exclaimed.

"That's an awful thing to say!" Zoe protested, her voice rising. "Di's a fine person. A fine *Christian* woman. Nobody gives more time to the church, and you know it."

"That doesn't mean she'll be a good wife and stepmother. I've known her all my life, and there's always been something about her. A coolness, as if she were living on a mountaintop looking down on everyone else. And she's a little too bossy for my taste. She's not the least like Mark's late wife."

"Now who's being a gossip?" Zoe said with a little pout. "Have you considered that Mark sees her in an entirely different light?"

Neither Zoe nor Ed said anything else for several moments. They were both too deep in their own thoughts to notice the young girl standing motionless inside the front doorway, some yards away from where they sat.

Lulu had come down from the playroom in search of her father. She wanted him to join the children in the playroom and play a game of *pachisi* with her. She'd heard voices on the veranda and was just about to step outside when Ed said, "It's a shame about Mark's wife."

This had stopped Lulu, and she'd hung back in the doorway. She knew she should not eavesdrop, but hearing her father's name, she couldn't resist listening for a bit longer.

She was far enough away that she could make out some, but not all, of Ed and Zoe's conversation. She was sure she heard Miss Zoe say something about the children getting a stepmother. And Mr. Ed said that Vi was getting "her hooks" into someone.

What did that mean? Lulu didn't know, but it sounded awful.

Then Miss Zoe sounded mad, and Mr. Ed replied so softly that Lulu caught only a few words: "wife and step-mother" … "too bossy" … "not…like Mark's late wife."

Completely unaware that he was being overheard, Ed was trying to raise another (he hoped less contentious) subject with Zoe. But a loud groan interrupted him in mid-sentence. He looked up to see a child dash across the veranda toward the driveway.

"Is that young Lulu?" he said, rising from the bench.

Zoe had also heard the groan and seen the flash of calico and blonde braids on the porch. Instinct told her that something was wrong, and she hurried to find Lulu. Ed was only a second behind her.

They discovered Lulu kneeling on the graveled drive. Her back was to them, and her head was bent over. She appeared to be holding her stomach and gasping.

"She's sick," Zoe said, running to the child. "Get Mark!"

In the next instant, Zoe was on the ground beside Lulu, wrapping one arm around the child's shaking shoulders and holding her head. After several minutes, Lulu's retching turned to soft sobs, and the shaking settled into a softer tremble.

"You're all right now," Zoe said soothingly. She rested her palm on Lulu's forehead and was relieved to feel that it was cool. "You'll feel better now. Ed is bringing your father."

This made Lulu look up with startled eyes.

"Not Papa," she said in a pleading way. "I was just a little sick. It's over now. Please, don't bother Papa."

"I think you'll be just fine," Zoe said with a smile, "but he needs to know that you have been unwell. He wants to take care of you."

The last person Lulu wanted to see at this moment was her beloved Papa. How could she explain herself? How could she tell him that she'd been eavesdropping and had heard something so awful and frightening that it made her stomach turn over? Lulu herself didn't know exactly what had happened, but those words — "wife and stepmother" and "not…like Mark's late wife" — has struck her with the force of a physical blow.

Lulu tried to stand. Zoe helped her up, placing her arm firmly around Lulu's waist.

"You're still a bit wobbly," Zoe said. "Stand still and get your legs before you try to walk."

Lulu wanted to get away, to escape to the playroom and pretend nothing had occurred. But she was still trembling, and her knees felt like jelly. She leaned against Zoe and let herself be supported by the young woman's warm arms.

She was feeling stronger when her father arrived, followed by Ed, then Vi and Elsie. Mark wanted to carry her to the house, but Lulu insisted on walking by herself. They went to the chairs on the veranda, and she didn't object when Mark sat down and lifted her onto his lap. She didn't resist when Elsie brought her a damp cloth for her face and a glass of water that bubbled with bicarbonate of soda. Lulu's still queasy stomach did feel better after the soda water produced a loud burp.

A Startling Conversation

Lulu was most relieved when her father didn't ask questions of her. Instead, he said, "I think the excitement of such a full day was just too much for your tummy. Miss Vi has gone for Max and Gracie, and we will be leaving soon. I want to depart while the sun is still high enough to light our way back to India Bay. Do you feel well enough for the ride?"

"Yes, Papa, I'm fine. Really I am," Lulu replied, making her voice sound strong. "I'm not sick. It was just the excitement, like you said."

Mark looked at her closely. Her normal color had returned to her face, and her eyes were clear. He touched her cheeks and forehead, reassuring himself that she showed no sign of fever. Her trembling had ceased, and she seemed altogether his healthy Lulu.

Grinning down at her, he said, "I believe you are all right, but I want you to sit next to me in the buggy. You must tell me if you feel sick again."

"I will," she promised.

A half hour later, the Raymond family was on the road to India Bay. Max and Gracie were surprised to learn that Lulu had been sick, for she almost never was. But then Lulu told them how she'd burped "as loud as an old bullfrog" after drinking the soda water. She spun the story in such a funny way that her brother and sister laughed and decided that she really was just fine. Mark watched her carefully for signs of anything wrong, but Lulu gave no further cause for worry. As the ride to the city progressed, she seemed a little quieter than usual, but Mark thought this natural. Her bout of nausea had made her tired. A good night's sleep and she'd be full of energy once more, he thought as he turned the buggy onto College Street.

CHAPTER

12

It Can't Happen

A happy heart makes the face cheerful, but heartache crushes the spirit.

PROVERBS 15:13

It Can't Happen

*L*ulu was the first of the children to come to breakfast the next morning. She seemed entirely herself, except that she ate more than usual. Mark was glad to see that her appetite had returned. He was certain that her sickness the day before had been caused by excitement and fatigue. He made a mental note to be on the guard in similar circumstances and watch his middle child for signs of over-stimulation. But he no longer worried.

Over their breakfast, Mark told the children more about Tansy and Marigold Evans. Max said it was very sad that the girls had been orphaned, but he also thought their story to be a great adventure—as good as any story he'd read.

"Those two girls are wonderful examples of the power of faith," Mark said. "To be lost in Wildwood for so many days? I know adults who could not have endured so well. When Miss Vi and Mrs. O'Flaherty found them, Marigold was quite ill, but neither girl lost faith in the Lord, and He rewarded their trust by placing them in loving hands. To survive on their own, they showed great strength of character and ingenuity."

"What's jen-u-tee?" Gracie asked.

"*Ingenuity*," Mark replied, pronouncing the word with care. "Ingenuity means inventiveness and resourcefulness. An ingenious person has the ability to find particularly clever or intelligent solutions to problems. People say that we are living in an age of ingenuity because so many people are inventing new ways to solve old problems."

"Like Mr. Alexander Graham Bell and his telephone?" Max asked.

"Exactly," Mark said. "Now, Tansy and Marigold Evans didn't invent a thing, like a telephone. But with God's guidance, they found the means to survive until they could get help."

This led to a discussion of other examples of inventiveness and survival, but Lulu's mind drifted in a slightly different direction. She was surprised when Kaki entered the dining room to clear the breakfast dishes. Then she realized that her father, Max, and Gracie were all looking at her in an expectant way.

"Are you interested?" Mark asked her.

"Huh?" was all Lulu could say.

Mark smiled and said, "I think you have been lost in a daydream, my dear. I asked who would like to go to Samaritan House with me this morning. I've promised to help Miss Vi with a new project there, and I'm meeting with her, Mrs. O'Flaherty, and a gentleman named Mr. Archibald this morning. Gracie and Max have agreed to accompany me, and we want you to come too."

Lulu didn't know how to reply. She couldn't scream what was hammering at her heart—*No! No! No!* She couldn't tell her dear Papa that she never, ever wanted to see Miss Vi again.

Mark saw the confusion in Lulu's face and thought he understood its cause.

"Perhaps you want to rest after yesterday's excitement," he said kindly. "We are just going for the morning. I told Miss Moran that we'd be home for lunch. You needn't go to the mission unless you want to."

"Thank you, Papa. I think I will stay home and rest," Lulu said. She could not tell him her real feelings about the mission and Miss Violet Travilla, so Lulu was truly grateful to her father for being so understanding.

Mark did not understand. He thought that Lulu's reluctance to visit the mission was caused by embarrassment. She was at the age when something like a sudden nausea can be a source of shame for a child. He had learned how hard it was for Lulu to show weakness. It might take another day or two for her to get over what was really a minor incident, but he trusted she would forget it.

Mark excused Max and Gracie, telling them to wash their hands and faces and be ready to leave in twenty minutes. But he lingered at the table a little longer with Lulu.

"Do you have plans for the morning?" he asked her.

"Not really," Lulu said.

"You can give Miss Moran a hand in the kitchen," suggested Kaki, who was balancing a stack of plates in one hand and pouring a final cup of coffee for the professor with her other hand. "She got a basket a' fresh strawberries from the vegetable man. She's gonna make shortcake for lunch."

"I'll go ask her if I can help," Lulu said, trying to sound enthusiastic. "May I be excused, Papa?"

"You may," he replied.

Lulu popped out of her seat and followed Kaki to the kitchen door. Lulu opened the door for Kaki, but then she came back to her father. She stood beside his chair, and shyly, she put her arm around his neck and rested her cheek on his shoulder.

"I love you, Papa," she said softly. "And I love Max and Gracie and Kaki and Miss Moran. I love our whole family. And I love our house, too."

Violet's Bumpy Ride

Touched by her uncommon show of affection, Mark hugged her and said, "I love our family too, dearest. God has blessed us, hasn't He? He has restored us to one another, and we are a true family with a home of our own. I thank Him every day for His loving generosity to us."

"You won't let it change, will you, Papa?" Lulu asked in the same soft tone. "You won't let our family change? You won't ever leave us?"

"Are you troubled about my trip to Mexico?" he asked.

"No, sir," Lulu replied. "I know that's your job. I'll miss you, but I know you're coming back. Miss Moran and Kaki will take good care of us while you're gone."

"You also have friends who care for you very much," Mark said, brushing a stray curl back from her forehead. "Miss Vi and Mrs. O'Flaherty will be visiting now and then when I'm away, and they want you children to tell them of anything you need. If you have any problems, you should tell Miss Vi."

But Miss Vi <u>is</u> the problem, Lulu thought.

"Is she your best friend now?" Lulu asked.

"The Lord is my best friend, and yours," Mark replied. "But, yes, Miss Vi is one of my best friends. Are you sure you won't come with us to the mission? I know Miss Vi and the others would like to see you."

Lulu was tempted to change her mind. In spite of everything, she enjoyed being at Samaritan House. She liked everybody there—almost everybody. She wanted to play with Jam and ride the elevator again.

"Not today, Papa," she said after several moments. "I want to make shortcake with Miss Moran."

With a soft laugh, Mark responded, "Then give me a kiss, and run along to your cooking. I shall look forward to

214

enjoying a delicious dessert with my lunch. Watch for three hungry Raymonds to return at high noon."

"It will be good, Papa. Everything Miss Moran cooks is good," Lulu said.

Lightly, she squeezed his neck and gave him a kiss on the cheek. Turning toward the kitchen again, she said, "I do love you, Papa, better 'n anything in the whole world."

Left alone, Mark thought to himself how precious Lulu was to him. He understood that his middle child was a complex person of many moods. Lulu wanted so much to be strong that she hid her gentle aspects. She was bold for so young a girl, always willing to speak up for justice, especially in behalf of others. Mark thought that there was an innate nobility in her selflessness. Yet he saw that her tough-mindedness was also a cloak of camouflage disguising a wealth of deep feelings that she didn't share—perhaps was afraid to share. The last few minutes with her had been "sweeter than honey." She had allowed her camouflage to slip and displayed an openness that was rare, and he hoped that it would be repeated. Silently, he prayed and asked his Heavenly Father for guidance in helping Lulu to open her heart and share her feelings.

Lulu always enjoyed being with Miss Moran, and this morning the tiny housekeeper's lively conversation distracted Lulu from her problems. In her twittery, bird-like voice, Miss Moran told stories about India Bay "in the olden days" that fascinated the girl. Lulu was especially curious about the tale of the ghosts in the big house that was now the mission.

"Do you believe in ghosts?" Lulu asked.

"The only ghost I believe in is the Holy Ghost!" Miss Moran declared. "Lots of people call God's Holy Spirit the 'Holy Ghost.' He's also called our 'comfort,' 'help,' and "counselor.' Now that's nothing to be afraid of, is it?"

"You have lots of faith, don't you, Miss Moran?" Lulu questioned.

"I don't think of faith as something that can be measured out like this flour and butter," the housekeeper replied, referring to the ingredients for her shortcake.

Kaki had just come into the kitchen, carrying her mop and pail, and she heard what Miss Moran was saying. "Jesus told us we could move a mountain with faith as small as a mustard seed," the young maid said. "You keep that in mind, Miss Lulu. A tiny little mustard seed movin' a mountain. It's faith that does the heavy lifting."

Kaki vanished into the broom closet, but her voice carried into the kitchen, "You're doing a good job slicin' those strawberries, Miss Lulu. Just mind your fingers."

Having found her feather duster and polishing cloth, Kaki left to carry on with her cleaning. Miss Moran finished the shortcake dough and let Lulu roll it out on the floured tabletop. When the pastry went into the oven, Lulu thanked Miss Moran for letting her help.

"You're good company," Miss Moran said in a jolly way. "Do you want to peel some potatoes?"

"No, thanks," Lulu said. "I'm going outside now."

"Stay in the yard, where I can call you," Miss Moran advised. "I want you to test the shortcake when it's ready."

"I will," Lulu promised.

Lulu removed her kitchen apron, now dotted with red splashes of strawberry juice, and laid it neatly over a chair.

It Can't Happen

Then she left by the back door, heading toward the hidey-hole behind the stable.

It was a hot day, and the sun beat down on her head as she crossed the yard and the small pasture. Her braids felt heavy against her neck, and her starched pinafore was scratchy against her arms. But when she crawled through the hole in the boxwood cave, she was relieved that the shelter was much cooler than outside.

Lulu sat down and removed her shoes and long cotton stockings. She had a lot to think about, and she intended to be entirely logical. For that, she needed to be comfortable. She crossed her legs, rested her elbows on her knees, and held her chin on her hands.

She closed her eyes, and instantly the image of a pretty young woman with dark hair and velvety dark eyes filled her mind. She heard the words that Mr. Edward had spoken the day before: "wife and stepmother."

"Not *my* stepmother!" Lulu declared. "Not ever!"

The ground was hard, even under its coating of straw, and Lulu shifted a bit.

How can I stop all this? she asked herself. *I can't do anything that would hurt Papa. Or Max or Gracie. Oh, Max would be so mad at me if he knew what I'm thinking. He and Gracie like Miss Vi. But they just don't understand! If Papa marries Miss Vi, she'll take him away from us. That's what happened before. Papa married our Mamma, and we got born, and then he went away. He wasn't gone all the time, but he wasn't like a real father to us — not like now. But we had our Mamma then. Our real Mamma who loved us, so it wasn't so bad.*

Lulu rolled over onto her stomach. There was just enough room in the hidey-hole for her to lie full length.

Violet's Bumpy Ride

Miss Vi isn't our mother. She's nice to us, but she can't love us like a real mother. She's got her dumb old mission, and she cares more about that. She cares more about that stupid house and those stupid poor people than anything. She'll take Papa away from us again. I just know she will! And I won't let it happen!

Hot tears were rolling down her cheeks, and she dashed them away with her fist. Lulu's angry thoughts were far from logical; her reasoning would have made very little sense to anyone who did not understand her deepest fears. Nothing about Miss Vi justified her anger. In fact, Lulu had to rely on her imagination to manufacture its own excuses to resent Miss Vi—just as she had imagined Vi's appearance before meeting her in person. If she allowed herself to think of Vi as the real person she was—kind, thoughtful, caring, unselfish—the truth would undermine her resentment.

Poor Lulu was convinced that if she were weak in any way, her world would crumble. The wonderful life they now had with their Papa would disappear. If he loved Miss Vi, there would be little love left over for his three children. It would be too cruel. It would be like living with Aunt Gert, but much, much worse because they would know that their father loved his new wife better than them.

In frustration, Lulu kicked her bare feet against the ground and pressed her forehead into the rough straw. Had there ever been a child who created so much misery for herself? Was there ever a girl so much in need of a perfect Friend to share her fears and soothe her sorrows? But Lulu didn't believe that such a Friend could care about her. Jesus, she thought, only loved good people like Gracie and Max and their Papa.

She remembered words from the Bible, "the LORD looks at the heart." Her own heart, she believed, was so dark that no one could love it, especially not God. The tears returned, stinging her eyes, and she wept until she felt as if she couldn't breathe. Then the storm passed, and Lulu fell asleep.

She awoke feeling very uncomfortable. She didn't know how long she had slept, but the shelter had become hot and stuffy. She sat up and began to pull on her stockings.

After shaking the haze of sleep from her head, Lulu realized that she didn't feel so angry now. She knew what she would do to save her family. Maybe it had come to her in a dream, but all of a sudden, it was so very clear to her.

As she laced up her shoes, she said out loud, "I have to wait till Papa is in Mexico. I can't tell anybody. Max might guess, but he won't really believe it. I can't do anything that will really hurt anybody, not even Miss Vi."

Lulu crawled out of the little cave. She was brushing the dust and straw from her clothing and her hair, when she heard Miss Moran calling, "Yoohoo! Lulu!"

Usually this funny little rhyming call made Lulu smile. Not today. Her mouth was set in an expression of grim determination. She had to pretend to be good as gold for the next two weeks, until her father departed for his Mexican excavation. She had to hold her tongue and be nice to Miss Vi no matter what. *Just as nice as pie*, she thought without a trace of humor.

Then I'll be bad—badder than I've ever been. By the time Papa gets back, Miss Vi won't ever want to see him again. I'll make her hate me—so much that she'd never be my stepmother. Not in a million, billion years.

This plan gave Lulu no pleasure, but she was sure it would succeed.

Violet's Bumpy Ride

She straightened her skirt, and with some effort, she forced herself to smile. Miss Moran was calling again, and Lulu yelled out, "I'm coming!"

Satisfied that she looked all right—just a little mussed from playing—she marched purposefully across the pasture and toward the house that she now loved so much, because it was her family's home.

She might have been a soldier—a young, freckled-faced soldier going into a battle of her own making. She had never before felt so terribly, completely alone.

Nice as pie to Miss Vi....

What troubles lie ahead for Vi?
Will Vi discover Lulu's secrets in time?
Will Vi's happiness turn to grief?

Violet's story continues in:

VIOLET'S DEFIANT DAUGHTER

Book Seven
of the
A Life of Faith:
Violet Travilla Series

MCP
Mission City Press

For more information, write to

Mission City Press at 202 Seond Ave. South,
Franklin, Tennessee 37064
or visit our Web Site at:

www.alifeoffaith.com

Collect all of our Elsie products!

A Life of Faith: Elsie Dinsmore Series

* Now Available as a Dramatized Audiobook!

Collect all of our Millie products!

A Life of Faith: Millie Keith Series

* Now Available as a Dramatized Audiobook!